PUFFIN BOOKS

THE
LIMPING
MAN

Maurice Gee is one of New Zealand's best-known writers for
adults and children. He has won a number of literary awards,
including the Wattie Award, the Deutz Medal for Fiction, the
New Zealand Fiction Award, the New Zealand Children's Book
of the Year Award and the Prime Minister's Award for Literary
Achievement.

Maurice Gee's children's novels include *Salt*, *Gool*, *The Fat
Man*, *The Fire-Raiser*, *Under the Mountain* and *The O Trilogy*.
Maurice lives in Nelson with his wife Margareta, and has two
daughters and a son.

PUFFIN BOOKS
Published by the Penguin Group
Penguin Group (NZ), 67 Apollo Drive, Rosedale,
North Shore 0632, New Zealand (a division of Pearson New Zealand Ltd)
Penguin Group (USA) Inc., 375 Hudson Street,
New York, New York 10014, USA
Penguin Group (Canada), 90 Eglinton Avenue East, Suite 700, Toronto,
Ontario, M4P 2Y3, Canada (a division of Pearson Penguin Canada Inc.)
Penguin Books Ltd, 80 Strand, London, WC2R 0RL, England
Penguin Ireland, 25 St Stephen's Green,
Dublin 2, Ireland (a division of Penguin Books Ltd)
Penguin Group (Australia), 250 Camberwell Road, Camberwell,
Victoria 3124, Australia (a division of Pearson Australia Group Pty Ltd)
Penguin Books India Pvt Ltd, 11, Community Centre,
Panchsheel Park, New Delhi – 110 017, India
Penguin Books (South Africa) (Pty) Ltd, 24 Sturdee Avenue,
Rosebank, Johannesburg 2196, South Africa

Penguin Books Ltd, Registered Offices: 80 Strand, London, WC2R 0RL, England

Published by Puffin Books, 2010

Designed by Mary Egan
Typeset by Pindar NZ, Auckland, New Zealand
Map by Nick Keenleyside
Cover figures by Athena Sommerfeld
Printed in Australia by Griffin Press

ISBN 978 0 14 330516 3

A catalogue record for this book is available
from the National Library of New Zealand.

www.penguin.co.nz

THE
LIMPING
MAN

MAURICE GEE

PUFFIN BOOKS

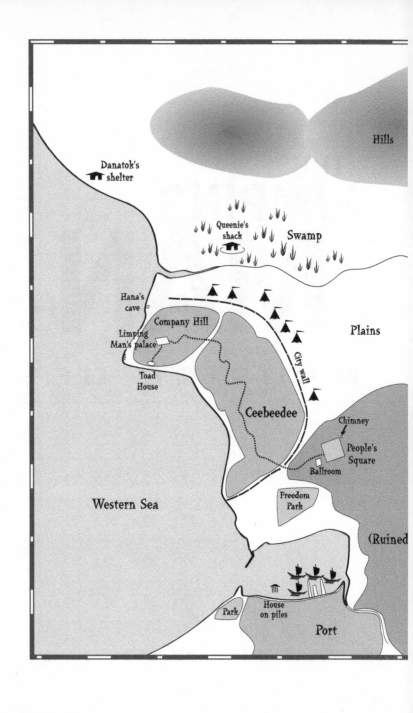

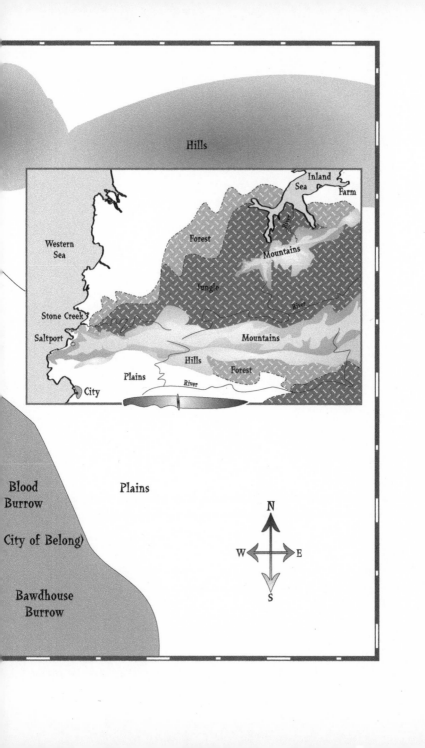

ONE

Hana ran through the broken streets of Blood Burrow. The smell of burning followed, sliding into her mouth as she gulped for air. It was as damp as toads. She would never wash herself free of it, and never stop hearing the women scream or wipe out the memory of the Limping Man.

'Mam,' she cried as she ran. Mam's smiling face, her shrewd eyes and careful hands, Mam bringing food and finding shelter and teaching her, always teaching, and always loving and always there – and Mam who had swallowed frogweed and was dead. Mam hadn't burned. Unlike the others she had found time to chew and swallow. She hadn't burned.

Hana had woken that morning to the cries of men in the streets, the screams of women and the wailing of children. Her mother came bursting into the shelter with the dawn sun streaming behind her, and wrenched the sack across the entrance. She turned and screamed, 'Hana, run.'

'Mam?' Hana cried.

'Into the crawl. Get as far away as you can. Don't stop.' With one hand she jerked Hana from her sleeping place, with the other clawed a fistful of weed from its pot on the shelf. She stuffed it in her mouth.

'Mam,' Hana shrieked.

Her mother forced her down, rolled her with her foot into the crawl. 'Go. The Limping Man,' she cried, with green froth dripping from her chin. She snatched more weed. There was terror in her eyes. 'Hana, they'll burn you.'

Hana went into the crawl, scraping her head, bruising her knees. 'Mam, come with me,' she screamed. But already her mother was rolling the stone across the entrance. Her mouth was foaming and the bite of the poison made her groan, but her eyes were as bright as embers and she said, in her own clear voice: 'Hana, live. Don't ever come back.'

Stone grated on stone. The hole closed. Hana heard the shouts of men in the room. She heard Mam scream and knew she had drawn her knife and run at them. Then she heard her fall and knew her mother was dead. The frogweed, the old women said, killed in twenty breaths.

Hana lay still, biting her hands to keep her terror and grief from breaking out. Men's voices, panting, the clank of body armour, the hiss of swords sliding into scabbards, were less than a body-length away. A dog, if they had dogs, would sniff her out. But there was only the sound of tearing wood as the constables kicked down the sleeping bench in the corner, and the crack of pottery as they ground the mug and dish Hana had shared with her mother into the floor. Then the swish of the sack door pushed aside and the voice of a man in command: 'This is her? The queen witch? You let her die?'

'Captain, she ate the frogweed,' a thick-tongued burrows voice replied.

'He wanted her alive.'

'Sir, she ran from us. She went down holes we could not follow.'

'Where's the girl? She had a daughter always at her side.'

'No girl, sir. No one else.'

'You were too slow. He'll have you whipped. Bring this one. He'll burn her anyway.'

Hana heard them drag her mother out of the shelter. She heard the clop of horse hooves and the creak and rumble of a cart and the thumping sound of Mam's body thrown on the wooden tray. Women in the cart wailed and cried her name: 'Stella, oh Stella, love.' She recognised Morna's voice and Deely's voice and thought: He's got them all. He had killed her mother. He had taken all her mother's friends for burning.

Hana curled up tighter in the crawl. She pressed her arms and legs into herself, trying to shrink to nothing, to sink into the stone. She sobbed silently, and when the cart had rumbled away and the voices were gone, sobbed aloud. She did not know how long she lay on the cold floor, but realised, later, that she had slept, and she cried out with horror that she had allowed herself that escape, with her mother dead and her friends taken. She saw how Mam had saved her. There was room in the crawl for Mam, she could have come, but then there would have been no time to roll the stone across and hide the entrance. She had saved Hana, and died by frogweed rather than burn.

Hana lay curled up for a long time. She had no strength to move, although Mam's words rang, and sometimes whispered, in her ears: 'Hana, live. Get as far away as you can.' She knew of no place to go. She wanted to stay near Mam even though she was dead.

At a time she judged to be noon she heard shuffling feet and hoarse whispers in the shelter. Scavengers had crept in and were sniffing and scraping in the wreckage. They would find Mam's knife – she heard them find it – and some rags of bedding and a shirt and hood and sandals worn through

9

on the soles. Little more. There was smashed wood that might be used on fires, and the iron pot sitting on ashes in the corner. No food in the pot. She heard their grunts of disappointment. Let them eat frogweed. The frogweed was still on the shelf. They went away and soon afterwards more whispering and creeping came, but this was a family, a man and woman and two children seeking a better home than the one they had. She heard the woman sigh with pleasure – this was a much better place. Hana wished the scavengers had left the pot and rags for her. A child whimpered and the woman said, 'Hush,' and at that sound Mam's voice spoke in Hana's ears: 'Don't ever come back.'

She lifted herself to her knees and her head struck the roof of the crawl.

'Rats. Quiet,' said the man.

'They might come out. You can get one,' whispered the woman. There was hunger in her voice.

They waited. Hana breathed softly, and after a while, as the noises of the family settled down, she crept away. She had only used the crawl once after Mam had shown her the way. Darkness had covered her like a sack, while the weight of stone pressed like hands on her back. She had felt she would never come out. Now she did not care. Tears fell on her hands as she crept.

Some way along she slept again and when she came out stars were blinking in the sky. She found water in the gutter of a fallen roof and drank. Dirty water. It did not matter. Nothing mattered now, even Mam's order, get away. There was nowhere to get away to. Fires glowed in the ruins, with people moving round them, families perhaps – but even those with children would not welcome her. They did not have enough for themselves and kept the warmth of their fires guarded from strangers.

Hana turned back to the crawl, then turned away. Mam had used it and her smell was there. It smelled of Mam alive, and Mam was dead. Hana held her close in her mind, and let her go, and held her close again, but each time the grief of parting set harder, until it was a stone in her chest, it was a heart that refused to beat.

'Mam, you were me and I was you.' But that was only true back in the shelter, on the bench they had shared as a bed, in the rags they wrapped around each other at night, and now Mam was a heart that would not beat and Hana was . . . What am I? The only answer she could find was: I'm alone.

She wept again, not for herself but Mam. That way she held Mam again, not inside her chest as a second heart, but warm beside the fire at night with a rat stew bubbling in the pot.

'Mam,' she sobbed into the night. Then she ran, not knowing where. In the daytime she might have recognised caved-in streets and doorways that led nowhere, but in the night they were simply dips and hollows. Tiredness overwhelmed her at last and she crept under the ledge of a fallen wall and slept, dreaming broken dreams, until hunger woke her in the dawn. She held her stomach, moaning, weeping but, after several minutes of abandonment, knew she must help herself or die. Mam had taught her how to survive, that was her gift, and the rest was up to Hana.

After hours of searching she found her way deep into the bowels of a ruined building and found a black pool, and thrusting her arm into a hole at the edge, found a family of drain lobsters. Ignoring their bites, she pulled them out one by one and smashed their shells on a stone ledge and ate the flesh. Soon she would find flints to make a fire and cook what she caught, lobsters and eels and rats, but raw flesh would have to do now. She would have to find a knife to defend herself and a pot to boil water so she would not fall sick, and clothes to keep her warm and a place to sleep. But where, where? She remembered Mam's words: Get away. Never come back. Did she mean out of the burrows? Hana knew no world outside the burrows.

She retraced her path into the daylight. Although she did not recognise buildings or streets, she knew from the smell of the air that she was in Blood Burrow. Her run in the night had taken her into the heart of the ruined city, away from the shelter she and Mam had shared in Bawdhouse Burrow. It was dangerous here, a man's place – the Limping Man's place. At the thought of him she was almost sick. He had killed her mother. He had taken all her mother's friends and today he would come down from his palace on the hill, with his armoured constables, and ride in a litter, high on the shoulders of a squad of leather-clad bearers, and call the burrows men to People's Square, and there he would burn them, the women known as witches – Morna and Deely and how many others? And burn Mam's body as well. Hana wept again, then stopped herself. No more. No more crying, no more tears. They were a waste. They helped no one. She dried her cheeks with her hands. She must think and plan, as Mam had taught her. She must go back through Bawdhouse and down to Port and then perhaps – she shivered – she could find the place called Country and go there. In all her thirteen years Hana had seen the sea only once and had never seen Country.

She made her way carefully through the ruins. There were women with pots and buckets drawing water from a well at the meeting of two streets, and children climbing in rubble heaps, hunting for edible lichens or – the greatest prize – a nest of beetles and a clutch of beetle eggs. There were men too, going to their work in People's Square. They would raise

12

timber benches, ten flights high, with a throne at the centre where the Limping Man would sit, surrounded by his guests and guards and servants, to watch the burnings.

Hana did not know how many victims there would be. Usually it was two or three but once, she had heard Deely say, it had been twenty, all women accused of being witches. The smoke that day, Deely said, had risen in a brown cloud and settled on the burrows and the smell had lasted until the winter rains washed it away. Deely's hands had writhed as she told her story, and tears slid into the wrinkles on her cheeks. Now Deely was one of those who would burn.

'There are no witches,' Mam had told Hana. 'There are only women who want to learn all the things that have been forgotten.'

'Like what, Mam?'

'Like how to stop the bone rot and the belly rash and the eye scale and the twisting in the gut that kills our children, all those things. And make plants grow and seeds not die and the earth not sicken. And how to make walls stand and roofs not fall. And how to clean the ponds. How to make pots. How to make wheels. Ah, Hana, there are so many things. How to breathe into hollow reeds and make the sound of birds. Music, Hana. You have never heard music.'

'I hear birds. But there aren't many. Only crows.'

'The birds are gone. But I remember women breathing through reeds and men beating drums – and it is lost. The Limping Man has taken it away.'

'Why, Mam?'

'Because . . . because he wants to leave no place for us to go. There must be no room in our heads for anything but him.'

'Where is he? Can I see the Limping Man?'

'No, Hana. No. Never go near him. He will take you by

your throat and never let you go. Or he will burn you.'

Hana remembered every word of that conversation and every sad and fierce expression on Mam's face.

'There's a circle round him, Hana, as wide as his mind can reach. Never go inside. If you do he'll find you and he'll hold you forever. He'll make you love him. He can do that.'

Hana did not believe it. I'll see him, she thought, I'll see him now and he won't see me. Then I'll get away. And one day I'll come back . . . She spat like a wildcat into a corner. She melted into the shadows and came out in an alley empty of people. She and Mam had explored Blood Burrow several years before, on a day when the men had been called to the hill to worship the Limping Man. They had travelled by a roundabout way to People's Square where Mam knew a hiding place. She had wanted to see where the witches were burned and, Hana realised, perform a ritual of sorrow and remembrance inside herself. Hana had memorised every hollow and crawlway, and she set herself to find them now. Mam's voice guided her: 'This way, Hana, under these beams. Now, jump, you can do it. This was a stable once, see the hay rack, see the chain.' Hana found it again and crept through. The chain was gone. Then, 'Quiet now,' Mam had whispered. 'There are women here. See how they rest when their men are gone.' The women had lain like bundles of rubbish in the pale sunshine. Today there were none. They were in their shelters while their men went to watch the witches burn.

Hana heard shouting far away. She approached carefully until only a row of buildings separated her from People's Square. A doorway leaning like a drunken man led into a room that seemed to have no outlet. She slid behind a fractured wall and found a stairway leading down. At the bottom a room opened out, with stone walls and a paved floor and a broad fireplace set in the wall. Mam said it had

14

been a kitchen. There were worn patches where barrels of flour and salt pork had stood. When Hana wanted to know what those things were Mam could not say, they were words she had heard as a child when old people remembered old, old days. They were things long gone and forgotten.

Mam had led her into the fireplace, which was large enough to hold a horse and cart. They climbed – and Hana climbed now, alone, bracing her feet on the chimney sides. She rested on a ledge, feeling soot fall like rain on her head. Higher up, light as thin as a knife-blade cut the darkness. She climbed towards it and found the ledge she and Mam had balanced on. The light was cold when she put her hand in it. Outside, Mam had said, the chimney crawled up a wall on the northeast side of People's Square, then rose like a tower over gaping roofs. Hana put her face into the light. She peered through a crack in the stones into People's Square.

The beaten earth beside the pond was thronged with spectators. Every man in the burrows was there, and every boy on the edge of manhood. Some of the men carried boy-children on their shoulders. A few cooled their feet in the pond, where the rushes were trodden flat. Others threw stones from their pockets at the marble head, half-covered in weeds, that rose in the centre, beside an arm holding a broken sword. The game was to land a stone in the statue's mouth. Then money changed hands – the thin brown coins of the burrows.

Opposite Hana, new-built benches rose to roof height, with red-painted steps climbing to a platform where the Limping Man would sit on his throne. The benches were already taken by early comers and the seats around the throne by men dressed in ways Hana had never seen before and could not have imagined – men in robes of red and yellow and blue, in hats decorated with ribbons and feathers

15

and pieces of glass that flashed in the sun. Their skins were red or white or black – blacker even than her own, which must now be covered in soot. They were tribal chiefs from the south and east, come to see the witches burn.

Hana peered at them with hatred. Her eyes threw flashing knives of hate. Then she almost screamed, almost lost her footing in the chimney, as she saw the posts sunk in the cobbled ground below the throne, each with chopped wood piled at its foot. Six. Hana closed her eyes. Morna and Deely, and one post for her mother even though she was dead. Who were the other three?

A huge shout deafened her. It rumbled like thunder, then died away into the clatter and sigh of two thousand people falling on their knees. The Limping Man's entourage came through a gate. A phalanx of armed constables beat a path through the kneeling men. They used leather whips and the flat of their swords. Behind them walked the Limping Man's courtiers, men from the city beyond the burrows, then his generals in cloaks and shining boots and belts hung with swords in carved scabbards. The crowd waited on its knees, breath held in, ready to shout their praise when the Limping Man appeared.

Hana, straining for a wider view, almost fell. Soot whispered into the depths. She kept her grip on the edge of the crack and regained her place, bracing her hands and feet on the stones. She was aware of shouts in the square, with an underlying beat. What were they saying? Not his name, he had no name. They were crying 'Man' in unison, a word that rang with the sound of an iron hammer beating on stone: 'Man, Man, Man.' Hana could not see him. His banner, held high to catch the breeze, came into sight through the black hole of the Western Gate. Its device, a crooked line beside a straight, shone as red as blood on its yellow ground. Then

16

his litter came, borne on the shoulders of four men. The top was closed like a lid and scarlet curtains on the sides hid the Limping Man.

The constables beat a path. The bearers carried the litter around the pond and set it down at the foot of the timber steps. Others had carried the throne down from the platform and placed it ready. The courtiers and generals climbed to their places. A man – a giant of a man, dressed in black leather – raised a horn to his lips and blew a long blast. The crowd fell silent.

Two men, stick-thin, like insects, parted the curtains at the side of the litter and the Limping Man appeared.

No one helped him. No one touched him. The silence in People's Square was like the midnight silence of the burrows. The Limping Man placed a carved stick on the cobbles and levered himself to his feet. He stepped down from the litter and stood for a moment, making sure of his balance. Hana could not see his face. He was a small man, dressed in blood-red robes with yellow flames crawling upwards from the hem, and a cloth crown rising in folds and bulging at the back, where ribbons drooped over his shoulders like a waterfall. She had never seen a man dressed so foolishly. How could he hide? How could he get away when someone chased him? Then she remembered that he did not need to.

The guard lowered his horn and the people bellowed, 'Man, Man, Man,' as the Limping Man walked to his throne, helped only by his stick. At each dipping step he seemed to fall, then he righted himself and the people roared. They loved him for limping. They wanted to lift and carry him, but he progressed by himself; reached his throne by himself; sat by himself and settled his stick between his knees. Four new bearers carried the throne up the steps, where they turned and set it down at the centre of the platform.

Hana saw the Limping Man's face, and it was – ordinary. She strained her eyes – eyes that Mam had said were sharper than a hawk's – but still there was nothing to see, no strength, no authority, nothing in the mouth or nose or forehead, nothing in the eyes, watery and red-rimmed and pale, nothing to make people worship him. Yet the crowd, on its knees, continued its deep-throated roar of gratitude and love. She could not understand it. A round-faced little man with soft cheeks and weak eyes and a leg that tipped him sideways at every step, and yet two thousand people roared his name as though he stood so far above them that their arms, held rigid, their fingers clutching air, could never reach high enough to touch him.

He smiled. The crowd howled louder.

Then Hana felt something sticky crawling on her face like a midnight grub. It crossed her lips and paused as though looking for a way into her mouth. She shook her head to toss it away. A grub could not hurt her. She felt it on her cheek, then by her ear, and she released one hand from the stone to brush it into the darkness. There was nothing there. But the soft crawling continued and seemed to move through her skin and wriggle into her head. She gave a cry of fear and inched her way down the narrow chimney. This sticky touch must be the Limping Man reaching out for her. What had Mam said? He would make her love him. It was why the men in the square fell to their knees and spread their hands long-ingly and bellowed his name. He crawled inside their heads and made them love him. Hana felt the emotion seeping into her brain and she used all her strength to force it out. It was like someone tying her up. It was like a spider spinning a web around her. She fought it away with the memory of Mam.

She heard, dimly, the sound of the crowd die to a murmur. She felt Mam, like clean water, wash the Limping Man out of

18

her mind, but knew also that he had relaxed his demand, and that was why the crowd had stopped its shouting and she and Mam had won their battle. If she had been closer, down with the men in the square, he would have swept her away. Again she remembered what Mam had said: the circle round him spreads as wide as his mind can reach. Hana must have been at its very edge and had managed to keep outside.

She stayed in the chimney with her eyes closed until her legs and arms began to ache. She must go or she would fall. But her need to see Mam overcame her fear. She climbed again and put her eyes to the crack. Roars of delight came from the crowd. It took her a moment to see why. Waist-deep in the pond, a quartet of naked guards were drowning two men. Hana was sickened. She closed her eyes, blotting out the sight. She had forgotten this part of the ritual, but remembered how Morna had said the entertainment always began with the drowning of men who had lived with the witches. When she looked again the guards were wading out and two bodies floated face down on the green water.

A shadow fell on Hana. Claws scraped as a crow settled on the chimney. She knew why it was there: to pick at the bodies when the crowd was gone; to hunt for scraps of flesh in the embers.

'Go away, crow,' she whispered harshly, and reinforced it with a push of her mind. The crow flapped away, cawing angrily.

On his throne, the Limping Man was smiling again. His round mouth opened, his red lips slid, and his slanting teeth gleamed in the sun. He raised his finger to the black-clad attendant, who bowed deferentially. The Limping Man whispered and the man, the crier, straightened, puffed his chest and bellowed in a voice louder than his horn: 'Bring the witch.'

Over by the farthest gate the crowd parted and four men marched through, carrying something – carrying Mam. Hana almost screamed. They held her by the wrists and ankles. Her head hung back. Her hair brushed the cobbles. The men handled her carefully, as though she were precious and yet as though she had never been alive. They laid her at the foot of the steps leading to the throne.

It isn't you, Mam, Hana cried inside herself. And then more calmly: It isn't you. That poor dead figure in its scraps of rag wasn't Mam. Mam was gone, Mam was free. She floated in the air. She whispered in Hana's ears: Get away from here, my child.

There was no harm the Limping Man could do Mam.

Yes, I will, Hana whispered back. But I want . . . She meant that she needed to say goodbye to Morna and Deely.

The Limping Man had risen from his throne. He leaned on his stick and whispered to the crier. He spoke for a long time, banging the butt of his stick on the platform, and the crier listened with bent head. Then he stepped away and blew his horn. The hooting and jeering and cries of hatred stopped. 'Listen, men of the burrows,' he cried. 'I am the voice of the Limping Man and this is my word. Hear no other. Hear only me. I will feed and clothe you. I will keep you safe from the darkness rising in our midst. Do not go near the contamination. Do not listen to the witches. You have seen two men drown – two who broke the prohibition. The pond is wide. There is room for more.'

The crier paused and the crowd whooped and bayed its approval.

'I will find you. I will find all who disobey.' He paused again, then pointed at Mam with his horn: 'As I found her.' The Limping Man, seated again, gave a little smile and patted his cloth crown. 'She was the chief witch, men of the

20

burrows. She was the evil one who poisoned women's minds, and men's minds too . . .'

No, no, Hana cried, inside herself. All she did was try to find out how to cure sick people. How to feed ourselves, how to live . . .

'Now she is the poisoned one. She sought to escape me. She ate the frogweed witches grow. But no one escapes. I will burn her all the same and her evil spirit will feel the flames . . .'

'Mam, Mam,' Hana whispered.

Yes, my dear, I'm with you, Mam replied. Take no notice of these men. They're only making noises.

'Bring her followers. Bring the other witches,' the crier bellowed.

The crowd by the gate parted again and guards came through, leading five women on ropes tied round their waists. Deely fought and spat, Morna walked blank-eyed, stumbling now and then. The three who came behind were from another burrow. It was part of the Limping Man's teaching that there were witches everywhere. One was a woman who fought like Deely. The others were girls scarcely older than Hana. One wept as she was dragged along and one, the younger, darted to the left and right, pleading with the men who lined the path through the crowd. They jeered at her.

The guards stopped at the foot of the steps. Deely raised her eyes and saw the Limping Man. She spat at him. He smiled his red sloping-toothed smile and raised his hand.

'Tie the evil ones to the posts,' the crier bellowed.

Hana saw them drag the women to the execution place, where men with chains waited, and others with burning brands. Four men bent to lift Mam.

'That's not you, Mam,' Hana whispered.

No, I'm here, Mam replied, in a broken voice that meant

Morna and Deely were still alive, and the other woman and the girls. Hana turned her eyes away. She turned clumsily in the chimney. There was no way she could help. All she could do was run.

So she climbed down the chimney and ran through the empty streets of Blood Burrow. Behind her, in People's Square, the crowd roared and hooted.

Brown smoke rose into the air.

TWO

It took her three days to find the place called Country. She came to Sea first and passed between it and the broken buildings of Port. For one whole day, dawn to dusk, she scrambled at the base of cliffs running to the north. Sometimes she climbed, sometimes waded in the salty water. If the sea had been rough she could not have passed. Hana had learned to stay afloat and then sink and pull herself along the bottom while hunting for food in the ponds and underground pools of Bawdhouse Burrow but she could not swim for any distance. The sea frightened her. It might pull her out into the shining place where it met the sky. She was careful not to go deeper than her waist and drew back when small waves lapped against her chest.

Sea gave her food, creatures with soft flesh that lived in shells fastened to the rocks, and small fish trapped in ponds. They were saltier than the fish from the underground pools but did not have the taste of mud or need to have slime scraped off their skins. She crunched them between her teeth and spat out their heads. The only fresh water she could find was a thin trickle running down the wall of a cave where she sheltered from the midday sun. When she left the cliffs behind at dusk she was too dry with thirst to look for danger. She ran to a stream flowing from shallow hills and threw herself face down at the edge, where she drank until her thirst was satisfied.

Dusk was turning to darkness. She crept away, looking for a place where she might be safe, but found only a hollow between two mounds of sand. She lay down and slept, curled into a ball against the chill of the night.

When she woke seabirds were screeching and a hawk circled high in the air. She knew what it was. Sometimes a hawk had made a few lazy turns over the burrows, then flown away as if there was nothing to interest it. She watched this one fly away too, then set off on her journey again.

Country opened out on her right. It frightened her even more than Sea. There were hills, there were trees, there was a long green line stretching away – it must be forest – and mountains rising like a wall at the back of it. It was too big for her. There was nowhere to hide. So Hana ran, high on the sandy beach; ran for the whole of the day. She stopped only to drink from streams, following them back until salt water turned to fresh. She chewed weed washed up on the beach. But as she lay down to sleep that night she knew she could not keep travelling this way. She must find other food. She must find flints to make a fire. And somewhere she must find a knife.

Mam? she asked. But Mam was not with her any more. Mam was a memory and only her lessons would help. What were they? Be still. Be watchful. Think what you do.

'Thank you, Mam,' Hana whispered, and slept.

In the morning she turned inland. She saw no animals or humans and no sign of human habitation. There were trees. She had never been close to a tree. Some had yellow balls

24

hanging from their branches. Fruit? In the stories Mam had told about Hari and Pearl, stories she had learned from Deely, they had eaten fruit as they escaped through the jungle. Hana pulled off one of the balls, bit it cautiously and waited for a burning in her mouth. There was none, only sweetness, so she swallowed – and waited for a pain in her stomach. But the sweetness stayed, so Hana ate. She carried away one of the balls in each hand.

The next day she followed the beach, rounded a headland and saw a new beach running into a blue haze in the distance. She lost heart. The seabirds screamed.

'Birds, what do I do?'

The hawk, or a different one, turned in the sky.

'Hawk, tell me.'

No answer.

She found a place to sleep, dreamed sad dreams all through the night and woke with tears on her face. That day she did not travel but hunted below the cliffs and up a stream, looking for a place where she might stay longer – a cave, a hollow – and looking for the sort of stones that she might use to strike a spark and make a fire. None were hard enough. She found shellfish. She found more fruit. But she could not live off these forever.

She lay down in a sheltered place where the sand ran into trees but could not sleep. Stars came out. There had been only stars straight above in the burrows. These spread down the sky to where it met the sea. Stars in strings and loops, blue stars, red stars and huge yellow ones. What were they? Mam had never told her. Hana thought they might be alive and watching to see she came to no harm. 'Thank you, stars.' She turned over on the sand, following their spread along the horizon, then turned her eyes inland and saw another shining there – and that could not be. Unless one had fallen, a star could not shine in the trees.

A fire, Hana thought. People there. She wanted to burrow into the sand and hide, but night was the safest time to spy. When she knew exactly who was there, then she could run. And underneath her fear was the hope she would find women who had fled from the Limping Man.

She left her place at the edge of the trees and moved along the beach. She lost the fire for a moment, then saw it again, flickering beyond the crowded trunks. Hana had learned creeping as a way to survive in the burrows. Her eyes were used to the dark and even though trees were unfamiliar she approached without stirring a leaf or cracking a twig. The fire was burning in a small clearing and throwing its light into a shelter built on the far side. No one was there – no one in the shelter, no one at the fire, although a pot sat on burning logs, with steam rising from it. The smell brought saliva into Hana's mouth. She crept closer. If no one was here she could steal the pot.

A voice behind her said, 'Hana, you're welcome to share what I have.'

Hana squealed with fright and rolled to the side. She felt for the knife Mam had sometimes let her carry. No knife. She rolled again, sprang to her feet and started to run.

'Hana,' said the man standing in the trees, 'stay still a moment. Don't run away.'

It was a calm and patient voice. She stopped well out of his reach – but not, she remembered, out of the range of a thrown knife. She stepped behind a tree trunk.

'I don't have a knife,' said the man.

'How,' Hana whispered, 'how do you know my name?'

'You carry it with you. I heard it as you came through the trees. Now, you're hungry, I can tell. Come and sit with me and share my meal.'

He walked past the fire, stooped into the shelter and came out with two bowls. He dipped one into the pot and laid it on the ground. 'Fish stew, Hana. That's yours.' He filled the other bowl and sat down.

Hana watched him from the shadows. He was dressed in a hooded cloak, belted at the waist. She had not seen his face, but his voice was friendly, with words separated by a pause, as though he did not speak very much. There was nothing to do but trust him – her hunger was too great. She stepped into the firelight, then saw his hands as he picked up his bowl, and jumped backwards with a grunt of fear. The fingers were too long and there were only three.

'You,' she managed to say, 'what are you?'

'Just a person, like you,' he said.

'No you're not. Not a person.'

'Yes, Hana. Of a different kind. My people are Dwellers. We live in the forests north of here.'

She had heard of Dwellers. Mam had told her, although she had never seen one. Mam had said not to be afraid of them.

'Your mother was right,' the Dweller said. 'But I'm sorry. I'll try not to hear what you think.'

'Is that how you knew my name?'

'It sits on your tongue like a whisper. Now sit down, Hana. This stew is better hot than cold.'

She sat across the fire from him and ate thick pieces of fish with her fingers. He went into the shelter and brought out a jug. She drank fresh water.

'You know my name,' she said. 'So what's yours?'

The Dweller laughed, a creaky sound. 'You have a right to know. It's Danatok.'

'I can see your eyes. They're different too.'

'Yes. We see like cats. But that's all. Hands and eyes. All other things are the same.'

27

'I've heard your name. Mam told a story . . .'

'About what?'

'Men called Keech and the Clerk. And a thing called gool. There was a girl . . .'

'Xantee,' Danatok said.

'She killed the gool. You helped her. You killed Keech and the Clerk too.'

'Others killed them. But it's true. Xantee killed the mother gool. Pity was her weapon. Did your mother tell you about what came before? Company and Ottmar and Hari and Pearl?'

'The poison salt. She told me. There was someone called Tealeaf too, and Tarl and his dogs. But I only believe in the Limping Man.'

'Ah, the Limping Man. You're running away from him. Tell me what happened, Hana.'

'If you can see in my mind you can find out for yourself.'

'That wouldn't be polite. Besides, I don't do it very well any more.'

She felt his sadness, his curiosity too, and his need to know. So, between bites of stew and mouthfuls of water, she told him about Mam, about the frogweed, about climbing the chimney at People's Square and seeing the burning-posts stacked high with wood, and Mam then, carried in, Mam dead, and Morna and Deely and the others, alive, pulled on ropes to face the Limping Man.

'I climbed down and ran,' she said.

'And you've been running ever since. Where to?'

'Away,' she said. 'Just away.'

'There's nothing there, Hana.'

'There was nothing where I came from. Only Mam.' She would not cry. She would only cry inside herself.

Danatok felt it and turned away. He went into the shelter

28

and came out with two yellow balls of the sort Hana had picked from the trees.

'Bellfruit, Hana. Although I don't know why. They're more like the clappers in a bell.'

She had no idea what he meant, but bit into the ball he offered, enjoying the sweetness and the juice.

'The story says you were in the city, and now you're not, so you must have run too. This place is away.'

He smiled at that and seemed to agree. Then he said, Hana, but not aloud. He spoke her name inside her head. She was so startled she almost dropped her bellfruit. Then she was angry.

'Was that you?'

'Yes, Hana,' – this time aloud. 'You could speak if you wanted to.'

'I can speak. You hear me. What do you mean?'

'The way Dwellers speak, mind to mind, without saying. Over distances, Hana, many miles. Over the sea sometimes, over the mountains. There are humans who know how. Xantee knows. Pearl and Hari know. I can teach you if you like.'

'No,' she said. 'It's what the Limping Man does. I don't want to know that. I'll talk the way Mam talked.'

'I think she could have learned.'

'Well, she didn't. I don't want you to do that any more – go inside my head. Or hear what I think.'

He smiled sadly, and nodded.

'Anyway,' she said, 'you don't do it very well. That's what you said.' She knew as she spoke that it was where part of his sadness came from. 'But you don't have to tell me,' she added.

'You've told me your sorrow,' he said, 'so here is mine. It's smaller than yours, Hana. I've lost no one like Mam.

29

But what I've lost is the thing that made me Danatok. All Dwellers speak but my voice was one of the strongest ever known. Tealeaf was strong – she still is. And many others. But I could speak over mountains and the sea. I could speak with Tealeaf in Stone Creek as though she was sitting on the other side of the fire. No other Dweller had my strength. Only . . .' he paused and smiled, perhaps a little sourly. 'Only two humans.'

'Humans?' Hana said.

'Blossom and Hubert are their names. Have you heard of them?'

'No.'

'They're twins. They're the children of Pearl and Hari. Xantee is their sister. When they speak they chime like bells in my head. Or so it was once . . .'

'Do you mean they're dead?'

'No. But dead to me – and I to them. Hana, I need to be close. When I try to send my voice over the hills it floats away like clouds and disappears. Over the sea it falls and sinks. When you came here tonight I heard nothing until you were in the trees.'

'I didn't make any noise.'

'I mean your thoughts. When I listen now, and hear, it's like the buzzing of a fly. And when I speak I croak like a frog.'

'You sounded all right to me.'

'Because you're close. You're over the fire. But if you stepped back and went down to the beach there'd be only silence. I'm nothing now. An old Dweller who buzzes and croaks.'

Hana swallowed. 'How long have you been like that?'

'I don't count. Three years. Four.'

'How did it happen?'

He did not speak with his voice or inside her head, but watching his face she knew the answer.

'The Limping Man.'

'Yes. Him.'

'What did he do?'

'You've felt him, Hana. You've felt how he sucks people in.'

'I got away.'

'Not if you'd been closer. Not if he'd seen you.'

'Is that what happened? He saw you?'

'I'd be dead now if the sea hadn't helped.'

He told Hana his story: how he had lived in a house raised on piles in the harbour of the ruined city of Belong for many years after Xantee killed the gool. The humans in the city went on much as before – fought and starved, made little armies, murderous gangs, in the place known as Ceebeedee and in the burrows, and some grew rich for a while, then they starved while others prospered. 'Nothing changed,' Danatok said. He had grown sick and weary watching them, so he left the city and travelled to Stone Creek to live with his own people, the Dwellers, or by himself in the forests by the Inland Sea. There, one day, close by the sea, he heard Tealeaf's voice calling him back. There was a new ruler in the city. He had rolled Ceebeedee and old Belong into one. Dwellers who ventured there to find out more never returned. Go and find out who he is, Tealeaf said. So Danatok took a dinghy and sailed down the coast and into the harbour at Port, where he found his pile house unchanged. Belong looked the same, the burrows looked the same, a city of ruins.

Danatok scouted in the streets. When he questioned people, some could only say, 'The Limping Man.' There seemed to be nothing else in their minds. They worshipped him, they wore his sign tattooed on their foreheads. Others were afraid. 'Leave us,' they said. 'He will hear.'

'He built a palace on the hill where Xantee killed the mother gool,' Danatok said. 'I knew a way there through the drains so I went to have a look at this Limping Man.'

The palace was smaller than the mansions that had stood on the hill in Company's time. The skills for building were lost, along with all the other skills that had flourished then. The Limping Man's palace was like an upturned box. It had yellow walls painted with red flames. There were no windows, no way for Danatok to see the Limping Man. He circled the building, keeping clear of the guards, not probing with his mind. By now he knew that the Limping Man ruled by a combination of awe and mental compulsion, and the latter, the compulsion, made Danatok cautious. He did not want to fight mind battles with the Limping Man until he knew more about him.

Danatok retreated to the trees. There was activity in the palace: an open door, guards moving about, and in a moment a huge man came out, dressed in black, with a horn of shining metal in his hand.

'At first I thought he was the Limping Man – but he didn't limp.'

'No,' Hana said. 'He's the crier, who talks for him. I saw him in People's Square.'

'Then two little men as thin as sticks –'

'His servants. I've seen them too.'

The crier blew his horn. Four men carried a litter from a nearby shed. The Limping Man appeared, moving with the help of a stick. He sat in the litter and the bearers carried it along a path in the trees to a small square building beyond the place where a marble hand stood, pointing out to sea. Company had made it in earlier times. Danatok hid in the trees. He had felt no power emanating from the Limping

Man, he felt nothing at all. Perhaps in the building there was some ritual he performed or secret food he ate . . .

The crier opened a door. The Limping Man went inside. The door closed.

Danatok knelt in the trees, trying to work things out. Was there something inside that the Limping Man drew his powers from, some flame or magical spring or creature like the gool? There was a small window beside the door but guards were close. Danatok was afraid to control them in case the Limping Man became aware. But Dwellers, with their long fingers, could climb where humans could not, so he lowered himself down the cliff, then moved sideways like a crab and climbed again until the back of the building stood over him, rising from the edge of the cliff. A second window, small and round and open to the air, was set in the wall. Danatok climbed silently. He looked inside and saw the Limping Man.

'He's small. He's no bigger than a child. His cheeks are soft. His mouth is red, with teeth that slant backwards when he smiles.'

'I've seen him,' Hana said. 'What was he doing?'

'He wore a brown cap and yellow robes. His hair is grey and hangs down to his waist . . .'

'What was he doing?'

Danatok sighed. 'He was feeding his toads. That's why he smiled.'

The room was lit by lanterns hanging from the ceiling. A wide trough ran along one wall, with rocks like islands in the green water and swamp ferns growing at the edge. Toads rested on the rocks or lay half hidden in the ferns. On the other side were cages of insects and tanks of tadpoles and small frogs. The Limping Man opened a cage and caught a fly in his hand. He held it by the wings and offered it to a toad – 'Big toads, as big as my hand,' Danatok said – who shot out his sticky tongue and gulped it down. Danatok clung to the window ledge and watched. He felt the Limping Man's enjoyment as he plunged his arm into the tanks and came up with frogs and tadpoles and fed them to the toads, whose sticky tongues, shooting out, were longer than their bodies. Last came burrow mice, kept in a cage by the door. The Limping Man held them by their tails and jerked them away each time a tongue shot out.

'He was playing a game,' Danatok said. 'The toads got the mice in the end.'

'Mam fried mice in a pan. They're good,' Hana said. 'Why didn't you grab him with your mind? You had the chance.'

'I was afraid.'

He could sense no place where he might take a grip on the Limping Man. 'His mind was like a handful of mud. It slid through my fingers. And while I was trying to find a way, he saw me.'

The two of them, Danatok the Dweller, clinging with his fingers to the window ledge, and the Limping Man, holding a struggling mouse by the tail, stared at each other. Then the Limping Man dropped the mouse and screamed like a squirrel caught by a tree cat. He turned to find the door, but fell without his stick and rolled on the puddled floor. The door burst open and the crier ran in. He scooped up the Limping Man in his arms and ran out, yelling orders as he went. Danatok tried to stop him but the crier too had a mind that could not be held. It was like a slippery stone. So Danatok scrambled down the cliff as fast as a jungle monkey and started north along the rocks at the base. Whatever it was that gave the Limping Man his enormous strength must be in the palace and the crier was carrying him there. Danatok knew he must get as far away as he could. He leaped among

34

the boulders, while guards with torches kept pace on the clifftop and threw down spears that struck sparks from the rocks.

Then the blow came.

'It was like a roof falling on my head,' Danatok said. 'I heard it rumbling as it came near. He meant to kill me, not just hold me.'

It knocked Danatok into the sea, where currents, running north, carried him out of danger. He had enough of his mind left to keep himself afloat. In the dawn half-light he crawled up a beach and into the trees and kept on moving north as well as he could, away from the Limping Man and out of the range of his crushing strength.

'No one followed me. He must have thought I was dead.'

After five days Danatok stopped running. He built his shelter and had lived there ever since. Sometimes fugitives from the city passed, but none who had seen the Limping Man as close as Hana had. They were the lucky ones who had kept outside the circle of his influence.

Hana did not want to talk about him. She had listened intently to Danatok's story but now that it was over she drooped. All she wanted was to sleep. Danatok offered his bed in the shelter but she preferred the warmth of the fire. She curled up beside it and fell asleep. After watching her for a while, and pitying her, Danatok covered her with a rug from his bed. He went inside the shelter and slept himself.

Hana stayed with Danatok through summer and winter and into spring. He never tried to 'speak' with her again but helped her build a shelter beside his. He taught her how to forage in the hills for edible plants, and in the forest for fern roots and fungi. He helped her weave a net from scraped flax and showed her how to cast it in the shallows for fish.

He showed her where to find flints to make a fire, which berries to squeeze for juice to drive biting insects away, how to use sponges from rock pools to suck poison from a wound, and many more things. How to pound bark into cloth and sew it with flax fibre, using a fishbone needle. How to make moccasins out of rabbit skins and knives from stone. So Hana learned the ways of Country and Sea.

At the end of winter, Danatok took his sharpest knife and cut her matted hair to shoulder length. He trimmed it from around her face. Hana looked at herself in a forest pond. She had seen her features only dimly before, in buckets of water, in half-lit pools under ruined buildings. She looked like Mam, but Mam's skin had been blacker and her eyes darker. Hana's eyes were green flecked with gold, her skin had the colour of the rust that ate the iron bridges in the wasted parks of Belong. She had never known her father. A red man perhaps, or reddish-white, one of those who visited Bawdhouse Burrow for their pleasure. Mam did not know which of many men he might be. She had only known how to stay alive – until she changed into a 'witch'. Hana snarled at her face in the water. She broke it with her hand and never looked again.

In the spring Danatok climbed a headland for seabirds' eggs. Hana would not join him. 'I like birds,' she said.

'Do you "speak" with them?'

'Birds can't speak.'

'Everything can. I've seen you with the forest birds. You listen and you hear.'

'I know what they're going to do next. But that's not speaking. All I do is see what they see. I did it with the crows in the burrows.'

'And the gulls?' Danatok waved at the screaming pack circling his head.

'They hate you. You're taking their children. They're sad too.'

36

'You feel it?'

'Yes, I feel. But they'll forget. Do you want me to tell them to go away?'

'Can you do that?'

'I think so.'

Go away, birds, she said. Lay some new eggs. And thank you for these.

The gulls screamed and flapped away.

Danatok watched her closely after that. She became aware of him probing in her mind and told him to stop. But she knew he kept examining her because, a few days later, he said, 'You're leaving soon, Hana. Where will you go?'

'How do you know I'm leaving?'

'It's time, isn't it? You've learned what you can from me. How to survive.'

She knew she could do that, but had no idea where she would go. Not back to the burrows. Never back there.

'Go to Stone Creek, Hana. Carry a message for me.'

'What message?'

'Say to them that the Limping Man is ready.'

'Ready for what?'

'To kill everyone who threatens him.'

'Do Dwellers threaten?'

'They do just by being what they are. They're speakers, Hana. But more than that, those with the strongest minds hear what others think. They can control them and make them forget. There are humans who can do it too. Hari and Pearl and their children, and many more, living in villages by the Inland Sea. If Blossom or Hubert told you to jump off a cliff you would do it.'

'I would not.'

Danatok smiled. 'It's lucky that in humans speaking seems to improve them.'

'Except the Limping Man.'

'Yes, him. He wants to be the only one. He burns the women he calls witches because he's afraid they'll learn to "speak".'

'Will they? Would Mam really have been able to?'

'I don't know. But you could if you wanted. You speak with birds.'

'No, I like them, that's all. How will he kill the Dwellers and the people at the Inland Sea?'

'Did you see men from the south at the burnings?'

Hana remembered them – men of every colour, in every kind of ceremonial dress. Chieftains, envoys from the tribes, seated on either side of the Limping Man's throne.

'He invites them, then captures them with his mind,' Danatok said. 'They become his slaves without knowing it. He sends them back to their people, where they raise armies. The tribes are assembling on the plains outside Belong. Soon they'll march north and scour the forests and kill every Dweller and human they find. Then the Limping Man will be safe.'

Far overhead, a hawk dipped in its flight, sending out a mournful cry. The gulls screamed. They felt Hana's fear and distress.

'Do they know? Do the Dwellers know?'

'I've sent messages and warnings. But the people who carry them are fugitives and perhaps they forget when they feel safe.'

'I'll go. I'll tell them.'

'Say they must leave their homes. They must hide and never come out until he dies.'

'What will you do?'

'I'll hide too. I know how,' Danatok said.

Hana left next morning. She wore a shirt and trousers and moccasins and carried a small pack containing a water bottle and food and a blanket and her rolled-up fishing net and flints for a fire. Danatok gave her his best knife. She wore it belted at her waist.

They said goodbye formally, concealing their fondness. Hana promised to seek him out one day. She refused to believe she was losing this friend, who in a small way had replaced Mam.

She travelled fast. She knew how to survive now in Country and Sea. She swam like an otter and climbed as though her hands were Dweller hands. On her fourth day three hills reared up in the distance, the middle one wearing a glassy scar on its face. Danatok had warned her against this place. Ottmar had mined his poison salt in the scarred hill. There was a town on the coast nearby. People had drifted back there to live. Avoid it, he told her. They kill strangers. Go around.

She headed inland, labouring in gullies and on slopes, and came down to the coast again north of the hills, where she rested for a night and a day. She wasn't sure she wanted to find Dwellers. Hana enjoyed being alone. But she knew she must deliver Danatok's message.

In the morning she climbed a hill back from the beach to work out the easiest way to go. The coastline was lost in haze. The headlands ended in sheer cliffs. She would have to keep inland and travel in the forest. It would slow her but there was no other way. She went to the edge of the hill to find her way down. High in the air, so high it showed no larger than a pond midge, a hawk turned and hovered.

'You could show me if you wanted to,' Hana said. She wondered if it was the same bird that had hunted in the hills and along the coast by Danatok's shelter. Probably not. Each part of this land had its own hawk. She watched as it glided out over the sea and came back in a circle that placed it above her.

'You are the same one. You've been following me.' She raised her hand in greeting. The hawk dipped and made a lower sweep. A small breeze ruffled Hana's hair, the same that stroked the bird's feathers in the sky.

'Come down,' she said. 'I can't fly up there.'

She felt a prickling in her head, as though a small sharp needle had stitched a thread.

'Was that you?' she whispered. Then she was dizzy and almost fell. The world turned over. She saw land and sea from high in the air and saw herself on the yellow hill, tiny, with an upturned face. Her eyes were green, her mouth open, her black hair tumbling. One pleading hand was raised at the sky. She saw, for a few seconds, what the hawk saw. Then it was over. She picked up her mind and held it straight.

'Hawk, that was you. You said hello.'

The bird circled lower, taking its time. Soon it swooped around her, with its head cocked sideways and its unblinking eyes fixed on her face. It had a white breast speckled with brown. Its wings were a shimmering green when it banked and were barred white and brown on the underside. Feathers on the tips spread like fingers. The tail, forked and tipped with white, twisted one way then the other as the bird glided in a circle round Hana.

Its beak was made for tearing and killing. Its eyes were hard and bright. They watched Hana as though she were prey.

'I'm too big,' she said. 'Anyway, you want to be friends.'

The hawk settled on a rock but kept its wings spread. Hana took a step towards it. The bird opened its beak and made a hard sound, like a snarl.

'All right.' She stopped. 'But we can't stand here all day. And you were the one following me.'

The hawk made no answer. Its eyes were so sharp she felt they could see her heart beating and blood flowing.

'My name's Hana.'

No answer.

'I have to go soon. Will you show me where?'

But words were the wrong way to speak with the hawk. She must do it with things, with images. So she asked the question again by picturing the boulder-strewn hillside dropping to the forest, and showed herself labouring down, as a bird would see her. Then she turned her eyes to the mountains in the north, where she must go.

'There,' she whispered. 'That's where I'm heading. Will you show me the way?'

The bird made no reply, but folded its wings.

'Well, I can't stay here all day,' Hana said. 'I'm going now.' She went to the edge of the hill and down a few steps, then looked back. 'Come if you're coming.'

She saw herself again as the hawk saw her, looking back, silhouetted against the dark forest. There was no discomfort this time, no pricking in her head.

'So,' she whispered, 'that's the way we'll talk.'

The bird sprang into the air and swept over her. It angled down the hillside, a long powerful glide, then climbed and flapped back to her, high in the air.

But all the same, you've got to have a name, she thought.

They went towards the forest, the girl striding through the scattered boulders, the bird circling above her and making every now and then its single cry.

She tried to respond. It was not an easy sound, but by the end of the morning she could make it perfectly. Hawk, it said. A lonely cry.

So, Hana thought, that's what I'll call you. Hawk is your name. Stay with me, Hawk.

THREE

A man with no name limped from the forest at dawn, carrying a baby in his arms. He passed through the village above the boats drawn up on the beach where a fisherman, setting off early to raise his nets, recognised him but lacked the courage to call the name that had once been his. The man climbed to a house overlooking the bay. He laid the baby down in front of the door, touched it on the forehead, let his hand linger, then limped away. Only a woman coming outside for wood to light her fire saw him pass back through the village. She whispered his childhood name and watched as he limped past the gardens and into the forest. No one else saw him and he never returned.

Pearl found the baby. She carried it inside and called Hari and Xantee, who was visiting while Duro was away on the summer hunt. Each knew, as Pearl had known, who the child was.

They've given him to us. Why? Xantee said.

They want him to have a name, Hari said.

And be one of us, not one of them, Pearl said.

Xantee fetched a woman able to feed the baby at her breast. Pearl named it Ben, the Dweller word for gift. She

42

thanked her son Lo and the woman Sal for their gift. She and Hari raised the boy as their own child.

He grew active and contented, but quiet. He could have learned to 'speak', but refused. He closed his mind and used his tongue, forcing Pearl and Hari to speak aloud so he might learn.

Why? Xantee said. Lo and Sal 'speak'. The people with no name can't talk any other way.

Perhaps that's why, Pearl said. And why Lo brought him to us.

Ben worked and learned beside the other children of the village. But more and more he turned to the forest. Hari taught him knife skills. At ten years old he hunted alone. At twelve he sailed alone along the shores of the Inland Sea and went inland from his anchorage for weeks on end. By the time he was fourteen he knew the forests better than anyone in the village, better even than Duro. Even so, there were dangers too great for him. He spent a whole night up to his chest in sucking mud and would have died if Hari and Duro had not found him. And the next time he went out a fangcat tore off his hand. Ben made it home, with the blood flow stopped by a tied vine.

One-hand, some of the village people began to call him. It did not bother Ben. He learned to make one hand do the work of two.

In the next summer he set off to find his father.

'We've been calling him,' Hari said. 'Pearl and I have called. And Xantee and Blossom and Hubert. We don't know if he hears or if he won't listen.'

'Why do you want him?' Ben said.

'There's a man in Belong, on the hill and in the burrows.' Hari shivered. The scar circling his neck showed whiter than usual.

'His name is the Limping Man,' Pearl said. She shivered too. 'Tealeaf says a messenger came from Danatok. The Limping Man is raising an army. He's going to march north and kill all the humans he can find, and all the Dwellers. He knows about us here.'

'Why do you need my father?' Ben said.

'Because Tealeaf says he's a limping man too. We know you were a baby when he brought you . . .'

'I can find him,' Ben said. 'He told me.'

'How . . .'

Ben would not say. 'What do you want me to tell him?'

'Say Tealeaf sent a message and he must go to Belong. Tell him what we've told you – the Limping Man will kill us all. And he'll kill the people with no name. But Ben, take someone with you. Take Duro or how will you find your way?'

'I know the way,' Ben said.

He set off next morning, alone in Hari's dinghy, and sailed south for five days, then east along an arm of the sea until he found the place where a brown river emptied its flow. He knew the way from a memory containing only pictures: an arm of the sea, a brown river, a mountain with a stone face that frowned, a red valley widening to a lake, and more beyond those, a trail of images leading to his father, whose hand had imprinted them as he laid the child at Pearl and Hari's door. If you need me this is the path, his hand had said. Also: learn their ways, forget ours until you need them. The child had little to forget, but the instruction beat in him like his own blood; and now, as he travelled, river, mountain, valley, lake revealed themselves. A wide jungle, thickening each day, lay on the other side of the lake. He made his way towards the rising sun, climbed a stone mountain with black uneven fangs and found a pass looping like a snake.

Two days to pass through. The jungle spread out again. Distantly, sunlight gleamed on water that had no end. There were no more pictures. Ben made a shelter and settled down to wait. Two days, four days, six. No one came. Now is the time to remember, Ben said. Softly, not using his voice, he whispered, My father. He slept in his shelter, leaving a fire of hardwood burning in the night. When he woke a man sat by the embers.

Ben stretched in the morning sun. He sat down opposite the man. Something touched his mind like a fluttering moth and he brushed it away.

'I speak with my voice,' he said.

The man jerked as though the sound stabbed him deep in his head.

'Does it hurt you?' Ben said.

The man opened his mouth. Ben saw his tongue move and heard a sound like branches rubbing in the wind. 'Like breaking bones,' the man said.

'I'm sorry, but you told me to learn their ways.'

'Humans "speak",' croaked the man.

'Some do, some don't. I'll "speak" when I need to.' He felt no liking for this man. 'Where's my mother?'

'She couldn't learn new ways. She told me to take you – home, she called it. Then she died.'

'Say her name. Say Sal.'

'I can't say names. No, don't tell me yours.'

'So,' Ben said, 'you did what she said. You took me home.' Then deliberately he added: 'To Pearl and Hari.'

The man made a sound that might have been a sob.

'Why?' Ben said. He felt another moth-like fluttering in his head and shook it out. 'No, talk like me.'

'I thought you might die too.'

'So you told me to be like them.'

45

'Yes.'

'I've done it.'

The man nodded. He sat still for a long while. At last he said, 'Your arm?'

'Fangcat.'

'You could have pushed him away with your mind.'

'I did in the end.'

'So you know how?'

'If I need to.'

'And you can "speak"?'

'I don't need that.'

All the time they had talked Ben had been aware of movements in the trees. 'Do your friends hear what we say?'

The man shook his head. 'They're not my friends, they're my people.'

'Tell them to go away.'

The movements stopped.

'Now I'll tell you my name,' Ben said. 'It's Ben. Use it.'

The man struggled with his tongue. At last he croaked: 'Ben.'

'And you are Lo. Say that too.'

'Lo,' he croaked.

'I've heard your tale, and my mother's, many times,' Ben said.

'Yes. The gool,' Lo said. He spoke even that name with pain.

'Now there's a man who's just as bad.' He told Lo about the Limping Man and the army he was raising and his mission to kill all speakers, human, Dweller and people with no name. 'Tealeaf says you must come.'

'Because I'm a limping man too?'

'So she says.'

Lo seemed to shrink by the dying embers. Ben watched him with pity. He felt an unspoken bond – this man was his father – but no love. It was too soon, and perhaps there would never be, for Lo was strange, with his matted hair and leathery skin and jungle smell and his twisted leg. He wore no clothes. He carried no weapon. He scarcely seemed human any more.

'Will you come?'

'The Dweller asks?'

'Tealeaf asks.'

'And my mother and father?'

'Yes. Pearl and Hari.'

'And my sister?'

'Xantee too.'

Lo sat hunched. He seemed to think, moment after moment.

'I ask too,' Ben said.

Tears rolled from Lo's eyes into his beard. 'You? My son?'

'Yes, Lo. Come with me.'

Lo nodded. He wiped his eyes and stood up. 'Wait,' he said and vanished into the trees.

Ben ate strips of meat and drank water. He pissed on the fire to kill the embers. Then he practised with his knife, throwing it at a tree trunk. He had learned to be just as quick and deadly with his left hand as his lost right. His toes were useful too. He could pick up the knife with them and flick it into his hand.

Lo came back. Still he carried nothing. They travelled through the looping pass and down the mountain into the jungle. Ben wrapped himself in his blanket to sleep at night. He did not know where Lo slept or how, or what he ate. He had trouble keeping up with his father, who leapt and climbed and scuttled, then waited patiently. They talked very little. Ben saw how painful using his tongue was for Lo. In the end he would take pity on him and 'speak'. In the end, he thought, he would love him too. Already Lo's oneness with everything around him filled Ben with envy. He wanted to be like that. But he wanted to be human too.

They came to the brown river. Ben pulled the dinghy from its place among the ferns. He was careless and did not see the snake curled up in the bow. The creature drew back its head to strike, and Ben had time only to think: I'm dead. There was no antidote for a viper bite. Time paused for a heartbeat as boy and snake faced each other; then moved again as the creature made no strike, but drew back its head, writhed out of the boat and rustled away in the ferns.

Ben turned.

You have much to learn, my son, Lo said.

Thank you, my father, Ben said. What did you tell the snake?

Lo smiled. It was the first time Ben had seen his face change in that way.

No magic, he said. I just told it to go away.

After that they conversed by 'speaking'; and Ben found himself acquiring other abilities almost as if he took them in by breathing. He found that he could remember the moment on the porch of Pearl and Hari's house when Lo had placed his hand on his forehead, although he had been no more than a month old. He remembered a voice that carried everything Lo knew and planted it like a seed and covered it over. All his life he had known it was there and not wanted it. He wanted it now. As he sailed the dinghy down the river, with Lo silent in the bow, he let the seed grow. Every now and then he said, My father? and Lo replied, It is so. By the time they reached the arm of the Inland Sea Ben knew everything Lo could teach him; and a part of what the people with no name knew. I'm two things now, he thought, but less than my father.

More and less, Lo replied. He meant that Ben was human while he could no longer be. He meant that he lived with the people while Ben could not, and although Ben might 'know', it did not mean that he could 'do'. But many things came to Ben, came easily, as they travelled. He found things to eat that no human knew about – a poisonous berry that, when wrapped in a poisonous leaf, produced a drop of nectar satisfying hunger for a whole day. Grubs that wriggled from the ground if a twig was snapped over their hole in a certain way. He baked them on a fire made from dead branches that burned when spat upon. Many things. He understood how the people made light, but he could not do it. Lo could, although not easily. He surrounded them with a yellow globe that kept the darkness pulsating beyond its edge. Ben tried, and tried again, and made only a flicker that slipped beyond his control and died. Then he slept for a day and a night, while Lo watched over him, smiling to himself.

They turned north out of the arm and sailed along the coast. Half a day short of the village Lo asked Ben to put him down on a beach.

Tell my mother and father to come.

Where?

Into the forest, Lo said. He limped away.

Ben sailed on. Late in the afternoon he pulled the dinghy on to the sand and walked to the house, where he found Pearl working in the kitchen.

'My father is waiting,' he said. He did not want to 'speak' with anyone but Lo. Pearl tried to hug him but he stepped back. 'No,' he said, 'I need to wash,' and he ran back to the beach and swam in the sea. It took away his feeling of strangeness and when he came up to the house again he was able to embrace Pearl and describe his journey.

She and Hari went into the forest next morning. Ben walked through the village and over a headland to the next bay, where Xantee and Duro farmed. He spent the afternoon working with them in the fields. Their four children worked too, chattering silently, creeping at each other with ideas, leaping with jokes, some of them about poor Ben, who could not 'speak'. He heard them but made no sign, only smiled to himself. He liked it best when the children laughed, which they did out loud. Xantee had taught them that laughter was shared and sharing was closer when everyone could hear.

'Will my brother see me?' Xantee asked.

'I don't know,' Ben said. 'Ask Pearl and Hari when they come back.'

They did not know either, but Xantee went into the forest alone that night and came back in the morning with tears on her face.

We spoke, Xantee told her parents, but it hurts him and he won't let me touch him any more.

Pearl comforted her. It had been the same with Hari and her. Lo was no longer the Lo they had known. But he's still our son, and your brother, she said.

That night they held a conference, Pearl and Hari and Xantee and Ben in the house, with Tealeaf and Blossom and Hubert joining in from far away. Blossom and Hubert were wanderers, close to each other but apart. Their connecting was like a flash of light. They roamed the forests and coastlines of the Inland Sea and the Western Sea, lived among Dwellers and humans with equal comfort and came back to the village frequently. They were not lost to their parents the way Lo was. Neither had taken a partner.

Hubert was far away in the northern mountains. Blossom was at Stone Creek with Tealeaf. They 'spoke' as if they were in the same room. Ben heard them but concealed it. Pearl spoke aloud to him the things he should hear.

A messenger came from Danatok, Tealeaf said. The Limping Man is massing his armies on the plain. All the tribes are there, southern and eastern and even some from the ice islands beyond the south. Danatok says they'll march in high summer and sweep as far north as Stone Creek and then come eastwards in the spring.

How can Danatok know that? Hari said.

Danatok guesses. He uses his good sense. But it doesn't matter when the Limping Man starts, he will come.

Why?

Fear of us. He calls us witches.

He wants to be the only speaker? Hari asked.

It's not speaking, it's control. It's power. He wants to rule every living thing, everything that moves. He wants the whole world to bow down and worship him.

Why?

Because he is who he is. I have no answer but that.

They talked on but could not think of what to do. Only Ben had a plan: I'll go there with my knife and stick it through him, he thought.

Blossom said: Hubert and I have tried to see inside him but we can't. We can't even see into the city. There's a fog lying over it, with the stink of swamps. It pushes us away. This man, the Limping Man, has huge strength. Danatok has felt it. No one who hears his voice escapes. He can kill if he wants to. He can make you worship him and hold you on your knees until you die.

Why didn't Danatok die?

There's a boundary. This power that he wields has an

edge. Danatok was there, on the edge. He would have died if the sea hadn't carried him away. But whatever the thing is that makes the Limping Man strong lives in his palace. Some magic thing –

There is no magic, Hari said.

Some thing, magic or not. Without it he's a man no stronger than any other.

Then I'll go there and find what makes him strong, Hari said.

No, Hari, Pearl said.

No, Blossom said. He would kill you like a fly. He would kill me if I was alone. He would crush me in one hand. And Hubert too, alone.

Hubert said: He's stronger than us.

They heard the sadness in his voice.

But if you go together, Tealeaf said.

No, Pearl said.

Then how do we fight him?

Not with our minds, Blossom said. Not till we know him. We'll creep into the city and be among his slaves and never 'speak'. We'll find out who he is, and what he is. Then . . .

Who will go? Hari said.

Hubert and I. But he's far away and we need to be quick.

I'll come as fast as I can, Hubert said.

Who else?

Our brother, Lo.

Why him? Hari said.

Blossom did not answer but Tealeaf said, Because he's a limping man. No other reason. The two must meet . . .

And he lives with the people with no name, Blossom said. The Limping Man will kill them too.

Listening, Ben thought: If my father goes to the city I'm going too. Pearl whispered to him what had been decided, and he repeated, aloud: 'If my father goes to the city I'm going too.'

'No,' Hari said.

'Yes,' Ben said. 'Lo needs me. He won't go if you leave me behind.'

He felt Blossom smiling at him, smiling in his head. She whispered silently, Yes, he needs you, and we'll need you too. But why are you hiding from us, Ben?

'Get out,' Ben said. 'I didn't ask for you.'

If you come you can't hide from us. It will be dangerous.

'I'll "speak" when I'm ready,' he said.

You're ready now.

'And when my father tells me.'

Don't be too long, Ben. We'll need every weapon we've got.

She had been speaking to him alone. Now she opened her voice: Ben can 'speak'. He speaks with Lo. When he's ready he'll speak with us.

Ben stood up. 'I'm going now. I'll sleep outside. I'll take a boat in the morning and pick up my father.' He smiled. 'I think he can make the breeze blow any way he wants. Where shall we meet? Ask Blossom.'

At Danatok's beach, south of the poisoned hill. I'll wait for you there, Blossom replied; and Ben heard.

He embraced Pearl and Hari and Xantee, collected the few things he would need – his blanket, his knife and water bottle and his flints for making fire – and lay down in the warm grass at the back of the gardens. The night was cloudless. Multitudes of stars spread their light, making the bays of the Inland Sea shine like the petals of a flower. Ben felt that he never wanted a roof over his head, or a bed or tables and chairs, or the touch of hands, and it made him afraid, for although he did not need company he did not want to be like his father. He felt Lo close; he had lain down somewhere beyond the hill.

My father, Ben whispered.

My son, came the reply.

There were other voices too, murmuring in Ben's head: Blossom, Hari, Tealeaf, Pearl talking in the house. The edges of their 'speaking' touched his mind as, half-understanding, he drifted to sleep.

The messenger, Tealeaf said, was a girl who fled from the burrows. She saw the Limping Man. Her mother was one of those he calls witches. She died of poison before he could take her but he burned her with her friends all the same.

The girl . . .

She travels with a bird. A hawk. She speaks with the hawk.

No one speaks with a hawk.

Hana does. She gave us her message and the next morning she was gone, we don't know where . . .

Next morning, Ben thought, as he slid into sleep, we'll be gone, my father and I . . .

FOUR

They sailed across the Inland Sea with a breeze behind them.
Ben did not ask if his father made it blow but he noticed that
when Lo slept it lost some of its strength. When he trailed
a line a fish took the bait after only a moment. Ben heard
him whisper as he removed the hook, using some word that
stilled the creature's pain. They ate fruit and dry food and
raw fish and drank from the sea. Ben could not imagine water
that was salt.

One night, before Lo took his place at the tiller, Ben said,
My father, tell me about the people with no name.

You name them when you call them that, Lo said.

How can I speak of them then?

Lo smiled – he smiled more frequently as the journey
went on. There's no way.

Who are they? What are they?

The jungle.

Ben did not understand.

They grew with it, as much as trees and ferns and vines,
and snakes and hummingbirds – and they'll die with it.

But they rule –

No. Lo spoke the word so sharply it stabbed like a blade. They exist, like every other part of the jungle.

But they can make sounds to keep animals away.

It's part of them, the way claws are part of a fangcat or wings part of a bird. The cat doesn't rule. The bird doesn't rule.

And they can make light.

It's part of them.

And heal.

They healed me badly. There's no magic, my son. They are who they are.

But why no name?

Does a cat have a name? Or a bird? But more than that, each one of these people, as you call them, is part of another until each reaches out into all the rest. They grew like that. The jungle made them. A name breaks them apart from it and from each other.

You're one of them –

No. The word was sharp again. I lived around their edges. I couldn't go inside. They taught me as much as I could know, which is almost nothing.

But you were happy with them ...

I was happy. I was sad. For a while I said: I'm one of them. Then I knew I could never be.

And my mother couldn't?

No.

She died – of that?

She died of grief for her dead cousin.

Mond?

That was her name. For a while she ...

Sal.

Yes, Sal – was happy with me, and with them, but when you were born she pined again, she wanted to share you with Mond and she could not. So she wished to die.

And the people let her?

It was what she wanted. I'm sorry, my son.

Ben gave Lo the tiller. He wrapped himself in his blanket and crouched in the bow, looking ahead.

You could have brought her to the farm, he said.

She wouldn't go. What happened was the thing that had to happen. I did what she asked me, I took you.

Ben stayed in the bow for a long time. The thing that had to happen. He fought against the words but could not change them.

Sleep, my son, Lo said.

Ben tightened his blanket.

This Limping Man?

What of him?

Will he kill the people? Will he find them?

If his army is big enough and has enough time he'll sweep through the jungles and drive them out, and outside the jungles they'll die.

Ben felt the sadness of that and lay thinking about it for a long time. Then he said, Tell me what they look like.

It can't be told. Sleep, my son.

Ben slept. Deep in the night the wind died and the sea stilled and Lo sat motionless in the bow, and in that time Ben dreamed . . .

. . . *trees heavy with moss, tangled in vines, with fat insects droning and lizards unblinking on the boughs. Cats creeping. Birds darting. Thin light leaking through the canopy. And here a flicker of movement as something not cat or bird, not snake or lizard, made its soundless way across the jungle floor, through ferns that touched like hands and heavy leaves that opened like doors. It did not trouble Ben that he could not see what it was. A small hand, monkey-pawed, curved round a branch. A foot, five-toed, sank in rotting leaves. An eye gleamed. Skin lit up in a shaft of sunlight and sank again like a stone in water. A whispering, soundless; a harmony reaching through valleys and winding down rivers and creeping as far as the jungle stretched, saying . . . Ben could not hear the message: love or fear or hunger or pain or satisfaction? The only meaning he could find was sharing. He heard as much as he could hear, and understood as much, which was everything and nothing. Everything because he was alive and human; nothing because he was not jungle. Yet there was no striving in his dream, no questioning and no disappointment, only acceptance. When it stopped he slept peacefully. The breeze mounted and Lo worked the tiller again and sailed towards the western shore of the Inland Sea, where dawnlight slid down from the sky behind him.*

Ben woke. He thanked his father.

That is as far as seeing goes, Lo said. To know more you must live with them.

Ben shook his head. He spoke aloud, but softly, so as not to hurt Lo. 'I'll stay who I am. But teach me how to make the wind blow.'

Lo grinned at him. That's something humans can't know. But bring me my line and I'll show you how to catch a fish . . .

They sailed hard all that day and the following night and came ashore in the morning by a river leading down to the Western Sea. It was too swift and rocky for their boat. They left it with Dwellers living at the river mouth and struck out south and west through open forest land. Ben was more at home in the silver trees than Lo, who was used to the dark and damp and heaviness of the jungle; but Lo had known the forest as a boy and each day he seemed to shed some of his darkness. Although still limping on his crooked leg, he began to stand straighter. He could walk from dawn to dusk and into the night, keeping up with Ben, moving ahead if he chose, while keeping all his senses alert in his jungle way. He smelled the sea before Ben and saw the different light it made in the sky and heard its slow sound beneath the breathing of the forest.

They met a river winding in its course. Far to the south a range of mountains gleamed against the sky. The place they sought, Danatok's beach, was south again, beyond the hills where the mountains ended. The river kept them company. It took on a yellow colour from the mud lining its banks. Sea tides reached this far, changing the taste from fresh to salt. They saw Dweller huts in the trees and lines of floats holding nets in the water and turned away, looking for the coast further south.

Lo, Ben, a voice said in their heads, and both, for a moment, refused to answer.

Lo. Ben.

We're here, Ben said at last. Where are you?

If you climb the hill in front of you you'll see my boat, Blossom said. You'll find speaking easier, Ben, with a line of sight.

She spoke as if he were a child, and he answered angrily: I don't need any help. All the same, he and Lo climbed until the plain of water opened out, shining like glass in the sun. Far out, a small boat with a white sail headed south.

I'll come ashore and pick you up, Blossom said.

No, Lo said. We'll travel on land.

The boat is quicker.

We'll be quick.

Lo, my brother, I want to see you. I haven't seen you since you took Sal away.

We'll meet at Danatok's beach, Lo said.

Ah, Lo, Blossom sighed; and Ben, although he stood

outside, felt the love flowing from her to her brother. He felt Lo soften and relent.

Speak to me when you wish, Lo said. We'll meet at the beach.

They turned their backs to the sea and travelled through the forest again. The mountains came closer. When they rested from the midday heat Ben found it hard to believe the ice on the peaks, whiter than the clouds brushing their tops, did not melt and slide into the valleys. He stretched out on the grass and stared into the sky. What a huge eye it was, watching him. He felt it saw into his head. The black dot motionless there was like a pupil. He blinked and wiped his eyes and focused more clearly.

Hawk, he said.

I've been watching it, Lo said.

It's watching us.

The bird turned in a slow circle, then broke suddenly and sped away south.

Now we must be careful, Lo said.

Why?

It was telling what it saw. And whoever it was speaking to is watching us.

Hana, Ben said. He did not know where the name came from.

Who?

Hana.

Then he had it: The messenger who speaks with a hawk.

Whoever it is, there's danger. The bird is diving.

What danger?

I can't see. Men. Hunting someone. Hunting her.

Lo stood up and moved into the valley of trees between him and the place where the hawk had disappeared. Ben followed, straining to keep up. He remembered Tealeaf's

60

voice reaching him in a dream: Hana . . . she saw the Limping
Man . . . she travels with a bird . . . next morning she was
gone, we don't know where . . .

He drew his knife and ran after his father.

Hana stood up quietly from the bed Tealeaf had made her.
It was the softest bed she had ever slept in but she did not
like the way the mattress – was that its name? – held her as
if it were Mam. No one, nothing, could take Mam's place.
She liked the Dwellers' food, but there was too much of it
and it made her stomach too full. She liked the Dwellers too,
especially Tealeaf; but snarled when she felt them poking
in her head. As for the woman, Blossom, who sat quietly
while Tealeaf and the other Dwellers questioned her, she
was dangerous. She was, Hana felt, like the Limping Man.
Hana knew as soon as she looked at her sitting on a stool in
the corner that whatever these Dwellers decided, Blossom
was the one who would say yes or no. She knew everything
– words before they were spoken and the things they meant
that the others might not know. The Limping Man would call
her a witch and burn her.

Ignoring her, Hana told Tealeaf everything: Danatok's
message, then Mam eating the frogweed, the burnings in
People's Square, her meeting with Danatok, Danatok spying
on the Limping Man and his escape – everything except her
meeting with Hawk.

'Hawk has got nothing to do with you,' she said when
Tealeaf asked.

The woman sitting in the corner smiled. Hana felt she
knew all about Hawk and she wanted to jerk the stool away
and sit her on her bum.

'I want to sleep now,' she said. 'I've told you what Danatok
said.'

Tealeaf showed her the bed. Hana tried it. Too soft. If she knew where Hawk was she would go outside and sleep close to him. But she had no idea where he slept – some tree branch, high up, or some ledge on a cliff. Each dawn she looked anxiously for him in the sky. He was always far away and did not plunge down to her until mid-morning.

Hana slept. Hawk was in her dreams. Blossom too. The woman was brown and dark-eyed and quick when she moved, but as still as a lizard when she listened. She did not laugh in her head, as Hana suspected the Dwellers did, but aloud, and softly, with a sound like stones rattling in a creek. The Limping Man would burn her in a slow fire. She was beautiful, like Mam must have been when she was young. She wore a brown shift, tied at the waist, and her hair in two plaits, but did not seem to care where the halves fell – both back or one curled on her shoulder and one on her breast. When Hana woke she whispered, 'Get out of my dreams.' She knew the woman had been poking in her head as she slept.

In the morning she took her belongings and crept away. Light showed over the eastern hills. Hawk would soon be on the wing, hunting his prey. She was nervous that if she was not clear of Stone Creek by mid-morning he would abandon her and fly away south. It had taken all her days of travelling to secure his trust. She had it now, and would not risk damaging it by mixing with Dwellers. By the time he looked for her she would be high on a hill, where he could scan the countryside before dropping down.

Hana went along the beach, past fishing boats lying tilted at low tide. No one was stirring. The sky was red. She ran south, keeping a steady pace. This was the way she had come the previous day, and found Blossom and Tealeaf waiting for her. Hawk had made his cry and peeled away inland. He did not like her going there. Now she whispered, Sorry, Hawk. I had to take a message for Danatok. And, something in her added, for Mam.

How had Blossom known she was coming? Hana stopped to chew some smoked meat from her pack. She shivered. The woman knew everything. She had probably woken and watched Hana creep away.

It rained that morning. Gusts of wind blew warm showers in her face. She enjoyed it, but wondered how Hawk managed, in the sky. Was he above the rain? Did it make his hunting difficult?

She turned inland at a little stream – again the way she had come – and broke clear of the forest and climbed a bare hill. The rain stopped; and there, in her head, was a picture of herself, tiny on the summit, looking up. It vanished and she knew Hawk received, for a moment, her picture of him, a small circling dot against a sky suddenly blue.

She had not felt so happy since before Mam died.

Hana and Hawk travelled south for several days. Neither decided which way to go, it seemed her steps and his soarings fitted on a string. But the direction was south, even though they struck inland when the coast was too broken for her to pass, and back to the sea when the hills were too steep. Hawk needed space for his hunting, he could not follow prey into the trees. He also took food from the sea, snatching with his hooked feet as he skimmed along the surface. Several times he brought her a fish.

She made a shelter and stayed for two nights, but headed south again when she sensed he was restless. And she too wanted to go south. Something beckoned her and she could not understand. Was it love for Mam or hatred of the Limping Man?

Just before dusk Hawk dropped down. He sat on a rock and folded his wings. He had never come so close. She approached until she could have touched him, and offered him a piece of the fish she had baked – his own fish. He did not want it. She ate, not watching him, leaning against the rock. After a moment she hoisted herself and sat beside him. His beady eyes watched her. She turned her head away, pretending indifference. Everything must be easy and natural, only then would they be true friends.

A movement at the base of the rock drew her attention. She had dropped fishbones between her feet as she ate and ants living under the rock were pulling scraps of flesh from them. Small red ants, busy ants, hundreds of them. Suddenly a door opened in the packed earth at the base of the rock and a dozen larger insects erupted into sight. These were scaly creatures, half the length of Hana's finger. She drew up her feet. They had claws like pond lobsters and tails with stings that curved over their backs. She watched, fascinated, as they attacked the ants, snipping them in half with their claws, scattering them with sweeps of their tails. They seemed to be infested with mites that ran across their backs as they worked and fitted into cracks in their armour and seemed to suck. Hana shivered. Everything seemed to feed on something else. The red ants were defeated, but some message had gone back into the nest, for suddenly warrior ants streamed out. They were larger, although not a tenth the size of the attackers. They moved so fast Hana could barely follow them, and could not work out what they were doing, how they were driving the attackers away. Then she saw. They were not biting the large creatures but picking off the mites infesting them, crushing them in their jaws, dropping their bodies on the ground. Once the mites were dead the creatures they rode became helpless. They did not know where to turn or where to find the trapdoor of their nest. The warrior ants butchered them. Only one, ridden by a mite between its eyes, made it to the hole. It dived inside and pulled the door shut with a flick of its tail.

Hana shivered again. How savage and bloody everything was. How dangerous. There were many things about Country, and probably Sea, she would never know. But then she reflected that her world, the burrows, was dangerous too, and just as cruel. It suddenly seemed to her that she belonged nowhere.

Hawk broke into her thoughts with an impatient cry. His eyes were still fixed on her. 'Sorry, Hawk,' she whispered. 'We all kill other things, don't we?'

He spoke to her in their way of speaking; and as though looking into a pond she saw her face, anxious and fearful, looking back at her.

'Is that what I'm like, Hawk? Not very friendly.' She blinked to get rid of the image. 'This is you.' Looking at him, into his eyes, she sent him his own picture, so clear it seemed to startle him, for he shuffled his feet on the rock and made his half cry.

'There, Hawk. We know each other now. Can I touch you?' She reached out and put her finger on the back of his neck and ran it down the silky feathers to the place where his folded wings met. He allowed the touch, although it made him shuffle again. After a moment she took her hand away. It was enough. It made their friendship secure. She would never need to touch him again.

In a moment he leapt into the air and flapped away. She made a place to sleep, well away from the rock where the insects had fought their battle.

Three more days they travelled south, keeping by the coast then moving inland. Hawk sat with Hana each evening before flying away. There was nothing she could give him in exchange for the fish or rabbit or plump bird he brought, but she always chose a rock well warmed by the afternoon sun.

The snowy mountains reared over them. They angled back towards the coast. Danatok lived south of the hills where the mountains fell away. Hana realised that this was where she was going. The further south they travelled the stronger the memory of the Limping Man became.

Hawk flew over the sea, so far away she lost sight of him. She climbed down stony hills deep into a valley packed with bush. A stream ran on a bed of pebbles. Her easiest way to the coast was to follow it. She doubted Hawk would come to her. He did not like places enclosed by trees, but she found a flat boulder in the middle of the stream and waited there, eating a haunch of rabbit she had saved from the night before. He would find her easily enough, and perhaps fly low. She lay resting on the warm rock, and saw the wide sea in her mind – Hawk's view – with a small sailboat foaming southwards in the wind. He swooped down until she had a picture of the person at the tiller. Blossom. She waved at Hawk.

He turned away. Hana was pleased. She did not want to see Blossom, and did not want Blossom seeing her. She found a seat lower down the boulder and rested her feet in the water. Hawk knew where she was. She felt safe.

Suddenly another picture pushed into her mind, making her jump and scattering her thoughts. Hawk was close, for she saw part of the stream she had followed, then bony hills above the trees enclosing it, the hills that had forced her to descend; and there, crossing them, two men. Hana looked for somewhere to hide. She wished she could question Hawk. What sort of men? Where are they going?

Hawk circled, keeping watch. The men found narrow strips of shade among boulders and sat to eat. One lay down and gazed at the sky. She saw with Hawk's sharp eyes: he was a boy. She shuddered as he stretched out his arms – one was chopped off at the wrist. His colour was reddish-brown, like her own. That was all she could see. Hawk was too high. The other man – was he a man? He was not a Dweller. His beard hung down to his waist. He wore a knotted cloth about his loins. She could not see a weapon; but saw with a shock of fear that he limped as he moved to a wider strip of shade. A limping man. But he was unlike her limping man – *the* Limping Man. No robes, no coloured headdress, no carved stick, no pink face. He was browner than the boy, no red in his skin. Although he dipped as he walked on his twisted leg, he moved easily. He lay down in the shade and seemed to sleep.

Hawk, she whispered. He went lower. And suddenly Hana felt watched. The man's eyes had opened – clear blue – and although he could not see her she felt he was looking through Hawk and finding her. She shifted quickly; splashed off the boulder into the stream; and suddenly Hawk's cry, far away, rang in her head – a cry she had not heard before but understood instantly: danger. A new picture sprang into her mind: herself, tiny, in the stream, and two men on the banks in front of her, and a third, thigh-deep, coming behind.

Hana slid down the silver rope that bound her to Hawk. She saw with her own eyes, which brought the men close as though they had jumped at her. A black man, a white man, dressed in leather jerkins with the Limping Man's emblem scratched on the front. One had the two lines tattooed on his forehead. Burrows men – she knew it from their grunting at each other, and from their smell as they came close. Behind her, the third man was city – he was smoother, white-skinned and used to command. Yet he held an iron knife, balanced in a way that showed he knew how to throw. Hana was used to running and hiding. But there was nowhere to go, upstream or down. The men on the banks carried crossbows. They grinned at her, waiting for her to move. The water slowed her legs and stones rolled under her feet. If she could get into the trees it would spoil their aim. She dived sideways, clawing at the bank.

'Shoot her. Shoot,' cried the man with the knife. She wriggled sideways and heard a bolt thud into the bank. She clawed her way past it, almost to the top. Then she heard Hawk scream and she flung herself round in time to see him swoop at the second bowman and rake his face open with his claws. The man sprayed blood but kept his hold on his bow and swung it upwards. Hawk hovered for a second dive. The man released his shot. Hana felt the pain. The bolt took Hawk in the wing, puffing out feathers and making him lurch towards the stream. Somehow he kept himself in the air, losing height, gliding between the enclosing banks down the narrow gorge. His feet touched the water where it heaped over a rock. He tried to flap. She heard his scream of pain. Then he settled in the water and floated out of sight round the bend. Feathers drifted in the air. One fell on Hana's throat. She raised her face and made a long bitter cry of loss.

The knifeman grabbed her ankle and hauled her into the stream. He put his foot on her and held her under, then jerked her up by the hair, let her suck in air and pushed her under again. The next time he pulled her up he forced her head back.

'Now, tell me your name.'

'Hana,' she gasped.

'Where do you come from? Quick.'

'The city. The burrows.'

'A runaway.'

'Kill her,' groaned the man Hawk had attacked. He was sitting up to his waist in the stream, trying to stop the flow of blood from his torn face.

'Where are your people?' the knifeman asked.

'No people,' she said. 'I'm alone.'

'She's lying. Kill her,' sobbed the wounded man.

'I ran away. I'm by myself.'

'We hunt runaways. All who don't worship the Man die. Say you worship him. Say you love the Limping Man.'

'No. No.'

'Kill her.'

The third man was crossing the stream. 'Let's have some fun with her first,' he said.

'Shut your traps,' the knifeman said. He was enjoying himself. 'Now, say after me, the Limping Man is Lord. He is Master.'

'I – I can't,' Hana said.

'And then I might kill you quick. Do you know who we are, girl? We're bounty hunters. See here.' He flipped open the cover of a pouch he wore at his waist. 'Do you know what they are? Thumbs, girl, each one worth a piece of silver when we get home. Runaway thumbs. Dweller thumbs. Seventeen in there. You're eighteen. But if you say "The Limping Man is Lord", then I'll cut off your thumb and let you go.'

'Ha,' scoffed the second bowman.

'Shut up, you. Now girl, you know what to say.'

'He . . .'

'He what?'

'He burned my mother.'

'Witch-spawn,' growled the wounded man. 'Kill her.'

'Yes,' said the knifeman. 'Enough talk.'

He drew his knife, took a handful of Hana's hair and forced her head back. The blade began a swoop, back-handed, at her stretched throat. She opened her mouth to cry Hawk's name. A thudding sound came, like the closing of a door. The man grunted with shock. He let her hair go and dropped his knife. Slowly he sank to his knees and fell face down in the water. Threads of blood drifted away from the blade embedded in his back.

FIVE

Ben threw without thinking. There was no time. As his knife flew the man's blade flashed in a crossways slash. The girl's face vanished behind his arm. Then the knife fell from his hand. He knelt as though his knees had been struck from behind and fell face down in the water. The handle of Ben's knife stood above the surface like a snapped twig.

The girl blinked. She opened her mouth, gulping air – gulping life into herself. Then she moved: jumped in the water up to her thighs, pulled the knife from the dead man's back with a savage jerk, scrambled up the bank, screaming a name – her own or someone else's? – to where the man with the bloody face had retreated. He was frantically arming his crossbow and he swung it up as the girl leaped like a fangcat, pointing the knife double-handed. She went over the weapon, making a spear of herself, and plunged the knife deep into his throat. Then she stood and raised her face to the sky. 'Hawk,' she screamed.

Ben looked for the third man. Lo held him in midstream. At some command Ben could not hear, he dropped his crossbow in the water. The girl, turning, saw him. She hurled herself from the bank, holding the bloody knife spear-like again.

Stop, girl, Lo said.

Ben heard the command. It held him still as though it was for him. The girl kept on until she was a dozen steps from the helpless man.

Stop, Lo said in a stronger voice.

She strained as though against ropes. 'They killed Hawk,' she managed to say.

'Give the knife to Ben,' Lo said aloud.

Ben saw how he strained too, holding both the man and the girl. He came up behind her and slid the knife out of her hand. Quickly he washed it clean of blood.

'Go to the bank. Sit down,' Lo said.

She obeyed, murmuring brokenly.

Lo looked at the bowman. He held him only lightly.

'What's your name?'

'Steyn.'

'Where are you from?'

'Blood Burrow.'

'The dead men too?'

'One's from the city.'

'Why do you come here?'

'We hunt runaways and Dwellers.'

'To kill them?'

'Yes. And take their thumbs.'

'Who to?'

'Our master. The Limping Man.' He raised his hands in front of his chest, thrust out his index fingers and drew one down straight, then the other, crookedly.

'That's his sign?' Lo said.

'The sign of the Man. We serve the Man.'

Ben felt the sadness in his father. He held himself ready

to throw if Steyn broke free. But Lo felt the danger and increased his hold.

He has a knife. Take it, he said to Ben.

Ben felt in the man's clothing and found a hidden knife. He looked at the blade, used for cutting off thumbs, and threw it as hard as he could into the trees.

'Now go,' Lo said to Steyn. 'And don't come back.'

'Can I . . .'

'What?'

'Can I take the thumbs? The agent pays . . .'

'Go.'

'I am a poor man. I must buy food for my sons.'

'Start running now. Go home. Never leave the burrows again,' Lo said. He repeated the command silently, digging it deep. Steyn's eyes went blank. He turned, climbed into the trees and vanished from sight. Lo washed his face in the stream, washing Steyn away.

Look after the girl, he said to Ben.

She sat near the bowman's body but took no notice of it. Her hands were red with his blood. Ben approached cautiously.

'Who are you?' he said.

'They killed Hawk,' she whispered.

'Tell me your name.' She was ugly, he thought. Black ragged hair, face stained with blood and tears, eyes wet and blurred. They were green, with golden flecks. He had never seen eyes like them.

'Killed him,' she said. Her voice had the same edges as Hari's – did that mean she came from the place, Blood Burrow, Ben had heard him talk about?

'Wash your face,' he said.

He turned away from her and threw the dead man's weapons into the trees.

Lo approached the girl. His beard dripped water. He looked as if he'd risen from the bottom of a pool. She looked at him with no interest.

'Her name is Hana,' Ben said.

'How do you know?'

'She took the message to Tealeaf. She talks with a hawk.'

'You use the bird's eyes?' Lo asked. 'He watches from the sky?'

'He's dead,' the girl said. 'It's all dark now.'

Lo turned away from her and looked down the stream.

'Wash yourself, Hana,' Ben said. She stank of blood.

She took no notice, but closed her eyes and rocked back and forth. Again tears ran down her cheeks.

Lo turned to her slowly. 'Say what you say to him. Say his name.'

'His name is Hawk.'

'He's still alive.'

'How do you know?' Hana whispered.

'He's in the water downstream. Run, girl. He's drowning.'

Hana ran through the trees close to the bank. She saw the one-handed boy jumping from rock to rock in the stream, keeping pace with her. He reached the bend and gave a shout, pointing into the cleft between two boulders, where the water broke into spray.

'Don't touch him,' Hana screamed. She jumped into the water and splashed past Ben, up to her waist. Hawk lay submerged in the cleft. The boulders locked his wings to his sides, while the weight of the water held him down. Only his head was free. His beak stretched upwards, seeking air.

Hana pushed her way into the cleft. 'Hawk, I'm here.' She pushed her arms around him, scraping them on stone, and pulled him free. He was heavier than she had expected. She could not fight her way out but lay helpless in the cleft with

Hawk in her arms. She thought they would die there. The boy, Ben, took her belt with his one hand and hauled her back. Slow and heavy, they came out of the cleft.

'No,' she cried when he tried to help with Hawk. She struggled to the bank and on to dry ground, where she sat and hugged the bird like a child.

'I'll make a fire,' Ben said.

Lo came through the trees. He crouched beside Hana and Hawk and looked at them without speaking. Hawk sensed him and opened his eyes. He clacked his beak weakly and Lo stood up.

'Where's he hurt?'

'His wing.'

'Let me see.'

'No. He's mine.'

'He's no one's, girl. Do you want him to die?'

She shook her head.

'If his wing isn't too badly hurt I can fix it. Let me see.'

'He'll bite you.'

'Not if he's asleep,' Lo said.

'How . . .?' Hana said. She trusted this limping man, who reminded her of Danatok, but she did not want him touching Hawk.

'I don't need to,' Lo said, and she started at the way he'd read her thoughts. He grinned and said, 'See, he's sleeping already.'

It was true. Hawk no longer strained in her arms. She waited a moment longer, then laid him on the ground with his damaged wing free. Carefully Lo spread it out.

'See, the bolt went through. It tore out a lump of flesh and broke the wing bone. The bird is lucky, it's a clean crack, it didn't shatter.'

'Can you fix it?'

75

Lo stood up. 'Keep him in your blanket. Wind it tight or he'll fight his way out. Tell Ben to get it. I'll be back by morning.'

'Where are you going?'

'There's a weed that grows where fresh water meets salt.' He made no other explanation but vanished into the trees.

Hana picked up Hawk and held him in her arms. Ben came back with an armful of dry branches.

'He's gone,' Hana said.

'Where to?'

'Looking for weeds,' she said sourly. 'He said to tell you to get my blanket and pack. They're on a rock up the stream.'

He was gone a long time. It was her chance to get away. These people had saved her, she would be dead without them, but she did not want anyone but Hawk. Yet if she ran with him he would never fly again. There was something about the man with the limp that made her believe he could fix Hawk's wing. He was quieter than the boy. He was stiller than the boy. She waited, breathing the forest smell of sap and ferns and listening to the soft rattle of pebbles in the stream. Hawk slept on.

'There,' Ben said, putting her pack down in front of her.

'What took you so long?'

He turned away. Something had upset him. 'I buried the thumbs,' he said.

'What about the men?'

'There's plenty of things that'll eat them. Maggots will. You'd better wrap up your bird.'

He watched while she bound Hawk tightly in her blanket.

'How did you make friends with him?'

She hid the fact that she did not know. 'Some people can do it.'

'He shows you what he sees.'

'Yes. I go up there.'

'What do we look like?'

'Nothing much. Like ants.' She remembered the battle she had seen. 'I could tell you only had one hand.'

He looked at her with dislike. 'One's enough. Why don't you wash your face? You've still got blood.'

She laid Hawk down carefully and went to the stream, where she washed and drank. Ben made a fire. Then he went away without a word. She sat nursing Hawk in her arms. How did something as heavy as he was fly? She began to understand his strength – and, looking at his beak, his savagery. You and me, she thought, and again she wanted to run. Only his broken wing made her stay. She put more wood on the fire.

Ben came back at dusk, bringing an eel and a forest pigeon. He cleaned them by the stream and laid them in the fire.

'Who is . . .' She did not know his name. '. . . the man?'

'Lo's his name. He's my father.'

'What . . . what is he?'

Ben frowned. 'A man. If he says he can fix your bird, he can.'

'He's like a Dweller.'

'He's lived most of his life with the people, that's all.'

'What are the people?'

'You don't know much. I reckon you'd die out here if you didn't have your bird.'

'Maybe. But I've got him. You haven't.'

Hawk opened his eyes. He struggled for a moment, then gave up. He slept again.

'Where do you come from? You talk like Hari,' Ben said.

'The burrows. Bawdhouse Burrow.'

'Where the whores live. You do it for a groat, that's what I heard.'

Hana hissed. She spat at him over the fire. He leaned back, grinning at her. 'You'll spoil the pigeon.'

'If I had my knife . . .'

'You'd do what?' From somewhere his own knife jumped into his hand. Then, just as quickly, it vanished. 'No chance, Hana. Now put the bird down and eat something. Try the eel.'

She ate. She would not speak to him. The eel was good. So was the pigeon. She saved a piece for Hawk. After a while she said, 'I've heard of Hari.'

'He's my father's father. Have you heard of Pearl?'

'Yes. They're stories. The poison salt. My mam told me that one. They're not true. Like the gool.'

'They're true. The gool's true. Xantee killed it. My father's sister.'

'My mam told them like stories.'

'Where's your mam?'

'The Limping Man killed her. He's not a story.'

'I want to see him,' Ben said. 'I've got my knife.'

'You're a fool,' Hana said. 'I'm going to sleep.' She lay down beside Hawk.

After a while Ben said, 'You'd better take my blanket.'

'No thanks.'

'Go on. I won't try and get in with you.'

She made a sound of disgust. 'I can sleep without one,' she said.

'So can I.'

Hawk woke in the night and struggled against his wrappings. She tried to soothe him but he snapped at her, cutting her hand. Ben squatted beside her. He tried feeding Hawk with scraps of pigeon. Hawk bit him too. They had no more sleep. Ben built up the fire and they sat close to it, keeping warm. The first light of dawn arrived. Tree trunks advanced out of the blackness. Lo slipped across the clearing and squatted beside them. He spoke a word to Hawk and the bird, exhausted from his struggle, slept.

Ben gave his father the food he had saved.

You need to sleep too, he said.

Lo shook his head. Bad things, my son.

'Talk out loud,' Hana said.

'Fishermen at the river mouth. All dead.'

'Humans?'

'And Dwellers. Two families. Children too. Dead.'

'With their thumbs cut off,' Ben said.

Lo nodded. 'The Limping Man's sign was drawn in the sand.'

Hana watched them. The boy, Ben, was hard. He fingered his knife. He wanted revenge. Lo dropped tears in the ashes of the fire. He was riven with sadness and pity. After a while he said, 'I talked with Blossom.'

'I know Blossom,' Hana said.

'She told me there are bands of hunters everywhere. Most come from Saltport but some are from the city. There are bigger bands too – twenty or thirty men. They kill everything they find. They call it cleansing. Everyone different from them. And every human who doesn't worship the Limping Man. They go before the army, scouring the land.'

'Has the army started?'

'Soon. It's nearly ready. Ben, my son, Hana' – he spoke her name with difficulty – 'it will flow across the land like a tide. It will drown everything. Drown and kill. Our world will never recover.'

'So if we kill this Limping Man what comes after him?'

'Others. There will always be others, whatever their names.'

'Not if the army doesn't come.'

'It will come.'

'It won't if we kill him.'

Ah, my son, Lo sighed.

Eat your food, Father. Then we'll go south, Ben said.

'Stop talking in your heads,' Hana said. 'And fix Hawk. That's why you went.'

Lo wiped his eyes. He finished his food. Then he motioned Hana to free Hawk from the blanket.

'Lie him on his back. Spread out his wing.'

Hana did as she was told. With his head limp and his claws curled against his breast, Hawk looked dead. She watched nervously as Lo took out his knife and knelt, one knee on either side of the extended wing. He shaved downy feathers on the underside, exposing torn skin and the ridge of the wing bone.

'I have to cut him now to see the break.'

'Will he feel it?'

'He's far away. He's in the sky.'

He sliced along the bone and peeled back skin and flesh. The bone shone white. A jagged fracture ran across it, open at one end. Lo cleaned the bone carefully. He put away his knife and used his fingers. She was amazed at how delicately they worked, baring the bone all round, then squeezing the broken ends together until they fitted.

'Now, Ben –'

'No, me,' Hana said.

'Now, girl. Feel in my pouch. There's some weed.'

She found the pouch by the fire. The weed was like a scrap of brown cloth and scarcely covered her palm when she smoothed it out.

'Tear it,' Lo said. 'Half of it.'

She tore it in half.

'I'll hold the bone together. Wrap it round the broken part. Good. Make it smooth. That's enough.'

She withdrew her fingers and watched while he fitted flesh round the weed-wrapped bone.

'The other piece.'

She laid it over the torn flesh, then watched as Lo fitted the flap of skin in place.

'In my pouch again. Some yellow berries.'

She gave them to him – a bunch of berries shaped like water drops. He squeezed juice from their pointed ends on to the wound, then on the edges of the hole the bolt had made.

'That will heal it. The weed will knit the bone.'

'Will you take it out then?'

'It melts away.'

'How long?'

'Two days. Three. He'll feel it. He'll hurt when he flies.'

'But he'll fly?'

'Yes.'

'Is that how the people fixed your leg?' Ben asked.

'They were too late with the weed. That's why I limp. This bird will limp. He has a hole in his wing. I couldn't fix that.'

'He'll fly,' Hana breathed.

Lo nodded. He turned Hawk over, folded his wings and helped Hana wrap him in the blanket. 'Now I'll sleep. Then we'll travel.'

'Where?' Ben said.

'Where do you want to go?'

'South,' Ben said. 'To the Limping Man.'

'And you, girl? Hana?'

'South too,' she said. 'Before he kills everything.'

'All right, south,' Lo said. 'I'll sleep till midday. So will Hawk. Then we'll go.'

He lay down by the dying fire and slept at once.

'Hawk would be dead if he hadn't come,' Hana said.

81

'So would you if I hadn't,' Ben said.

He did not like the way Lo had let her help, or the way he used 'Hana' more quickly than he had managed 'Ben'. He wanted to say, You keep your Hawk, I'll keep my father.

He put new wood on the fire to make its warmth reach Lo. Then he went upstream to a deep pool, slipped off his trousers and shirt and dived in. When he surfaced he saw Hana wading into a pool further down. They swam, taking no notice of each other.

SIX

They kept away from the coastal hills, where bounty hunters used the trails, and crossed by a mountain pass into the forests north of Belong. It took three days. Ben carried a load of firewood on his back, but still the cold slowed them and the footing in the pass slid them into icy pools. Hana had most trouble. She would not let Lo or Ben carry Hawk.

The bird fought to free himself even though moving made him utter his harsh scream, which Hana joined her voice to, giving him company in his pain. She tried to see what he saw but nothing came, although sometimes her own ghost moved behind her eyes. She began to feel they would never be friends again. When they stopped to rest she offered him pieces of the mountain birds Ben snared. After refusing for two days, he ate, snapping at Hana's fingers as she fed him.

Late on the third day they broke out of the pass. The distant sea was golden in the evening sun, with threads of silver running through it. A haze lay over the forests and the plains. Belong was far south. Saltport was west, hidden by the huge collapsing bulk of the mountain range.

'Where do we go?' Ben said.

Lo pointed to the coast. 'Danatok's shelter. Blossom will wait there.'

Ben grunted and Hana turned away. Neither wanted to see Blossom again.

'If anyone can face the Limping Man, she can,' Lo said. 'Hubert might be there too. The pair of them . . .'

'Hubert's in the north,' Ben said.

'He'll come. He runs where others walk.'

Ben shrugged, only half believing. He squatted to make a fire and caught Hawk's eyes watching him. He did not like the bird any better than the twins. 'He might be ready to fly,' he said to Hana.

Lo nodded. 'The bone should be healed. Try him.'

Hana was frightened his damaged wing would not hold him. She imagined it snapping in mid-flight and Hawk tumbling like a wounded pigeon into the forest. He watched her with his cruel eyes and clacked his beak when she came near.

'Hawk, you're my brother,' she whispered, kneeling by him so the others would not hear. 'If you want to go, go. But come back to me if you can.'

She began to unwrap the blanket.

'Take him to the edge of the hill where he can drop down,' Lo said.

She carried him to a place where the land collapsed into a shingle slide. Keeping clear of his beak, she unwrapped him. His legs fought, tangling in the cloth, and his undamaged wing rose like an arm. It flapped strongly, throwing him off balance and threatening to tumble him down the slide. Hana cried out. She grabbed at him.

'Leave him,' Lo said.

Hawk stretched his wounded wing and gave a screech of pain. He leaped into the air, but his left wing was stronger than his right and for a moment he slid on his breast. Then both his wings took air and he was free, with his drawn-up claws scraping the rocks. Down, down he went, no more than a man's height from the ground, until, with a tiny flap, he eased away from the shingle face. Still he seemed to fall, rushing towards the line of scrub at the winter snowline. Another small flap, both wings, and he made a clumsy lurch over the wall of brush, and settled into his glide again. They watched as he crossed the line of the forest, his back like a glowing spark in the evening sun – watched until the spark went out and Hawk was gone.

Hana turned away from Lo and Ben. She walked until she was hidden, not wanting them to see her tears.

'Hawk, you'll come back. I know you will.'

She sat by herself until the sky was dark. The land before her was like a pit. She did not want to go down into it. But Hawk had gone there and she must follow if she ever wanted to see him again.

In the morning they slid down the shingle, went through scrub into the forest and set off for the coast. They did not expect to meet hunters; the land had been scoured. Hana watched for Hawk but knew he had hidden himself somewhere. He would rest and heal his wound and learn to fly again. When that was done, would he remember her? She would watch for him, always watch – a hawk who limped as he flew. But here in the forest there was little point. Even if he came she would not see him through the tree cover.

Near the coast they were cautious again. Here were trails men might use on their way to Saltport. Lo 'spoke' with Blossom. The Stone Creek boat was making slow progress against a wind too strong for her to control. She had gone ashore on the north side of the three hills and spied on the town. There were boats at the wharves. She would have to take hers far out to sea to avoid being seen. And there were many men. Lo and Ben and Hana would need to be alert.

The poisoned hill still wore its scar. Blossom was pleased to leave it behind.

'Ask if she's seen Hawk,' Hana said; and heard Blossom's reply, a sound like running water, in her head: There are many hawks. Your friend will come again when he's ready.

Thank you, Hana said, not knowing if Blossom would hear.

They reached the coast next day. Hana recognised a headland where she had taken shellfish. And these were the skies where she had first seen Hawk. She tried to stop her eyes from searching. When he was ready, Blossom had said. It would not be soon. She concentrated on watching Lo and Ben. They knew the forest better than her. It amazed her the way Lo understood everything and was aware – a leaf falling, an insect buzzing, a fangcat prowling – and how he could speak with living things and hear their silent reply. And Ben, the one-handed boy, how quick he was, how deadly. She watched him hold his knife between his feet and sharpen the blade on a stone he carried. She saw it leap into his hand like a live thing when a fangcat snarled at them from a branch. Lo put out his arm, preventing Ben's throw. He 'spoke' to the cat and sent it slinking away.

Hana felt safe with them. At times she forgot the danger from the Limping Man.

They waited for Blossom in trees in the curve of a bay. She sailed in silently, appearing from the black night like a ghost. Ben and Lo dragged her dinghy deep into the trees. They scrubbed out the keel-marks on the beach. At dawn they started for Danatok's shelter, more than a day's travel south. They kept clear of forest tracks and the bare tops of hills. Twice Blossom stopped them and they hid while bands of men went by.

They skirted round places where killing had been done. The forest seemed no different but Hana began to sense what Blossom sensed – fair places, sunny places, that had become dark with the evil done there.

She began to be afraid for Danatok. Blossom grew anxious too. There was only silence when she tried to 'speak' with him.

'He can't "speak" any more,' Hana said. 'He can only croak like a frog.'

'I'd hear a croak,' Blossom said.

At midday they came to places Hana recognised – the pool where she had seen her face, the swamp where she had cut flax to weave her net. She went in front of Blossom, finding the path. Danatok, she whispered, remembering how he had heard her creeping in the trees on the night she had found his fire. The clearing opened up. She gave a cry. It was trampled flat. Danatok's shelter, and hers beside it, were torn to pieces. And here, on the ground, was the hood from his cloak, charred in the ashes of a fire. Blood smeared the stone Danatok had used as a seat.

'They held him down. Cut his throat,' Ben said.

Hana fell to her knees and covered her face. Mam dead, Hawk flown away, now Danatok. But Blossom, speaking aloud, said, 'There's been no killing. They must have cut off his thumb. They've taken him.'

'Why?' Ben said.

'Because he saw the Limping Man and got away from him.'

'They'll drown him,' Hana whispered. She ran down to the beach, where she searched the sky for Hawk. She needed Hawk. It seemed her courage depended on that black speck circling in the sky. But the sky was empty, and her heart was empty. Hatred of the Limping Man was all she had left.

She sat among the sandhills until the sun was low. Once she saw Ben on the beach, throwing a net he must have found in the wreckage. He walked up the beach carrying fish.

'You'd better come or you won't get any.'

Your knife won't be any good, she whispered to herself.

Blossom came later and sat with her and put her arm around her. Hana did not pull away. She trusted the woman better now but was sorry for her. She was like Hawk but not as strong.

'Everything gets taken away,' Hana said.

They walked to the ruined shelter in the dusk. All Blossom's abilities would be no better than Ben's knife. There was another world, away from this, where the Limping Man lived. No one could get in there and kill him. But he could get into Hana's world.

Halfway through the night Hubert arrived. Hana, wrapped in her blanket, saw him walk into the clearing and sit by the ashes of the fire. She heard his voice: Sleep, Hana, and replied grumpily, I will when I'm ready. She did not like the way these people walked into her head without being asked. She would get away from them, if she could, by herself.

She went fishing with Ben in the morning. She was comfortable with him because, like her, he spoke aloud. They netted a dozen flat-fish and cleaned them at the tide line under a roof of screaming gulls. She marvelled at the way his single hand did the work of two and the way his toes picked things up like fingers. He gathered wood and made a fire in the clearing. They cooked the fish while Blossom and Hubert and Lo walked on the beach.

'What are they talking about?'

'How to catch the bugger,' Ben said.

'They won't catch him.'

'Maybe not. I wouldn't sneak up, I'd go straight at him.' He seemed uncertain. Was he starting to see that more would be needed than a knife? And more would be needed, Hana thought, than Blossom and Hubert. She had watched them in the morning as they greeted each other. All they did was exchange a smile, and she understood they hadn't been apart. Hubert in the north, Blossom at Stone Creek, they had spoken as clearly as if they sat over a table from each other.

He was her twin, black-haired, brown-skinned. He moved like her, with the easiness of a cat, and understood her as she understood herself. As much passed between them in a single look as it would take an hour of speech to tell. Yet Hana had no wish to be like them. Although they must have a way of keeping some part hidden, they could never be alone. She would rather be like Lo, who joined with them and spoke with them but kept himself apart. If Blossom died or Hubert died the other would die too. It made her shiver. She had loved Mam as much as these two loved each other yet she had run and hidden and kept herself alive.

Hana knew, without being told, what Blossom and Hubert could do: command, compel, wipe out memory, make, if they chose, someone curl up and die. But even they would not be equal to the Limping Man. They could not be cruel.

'I'm not going to stay with them,' she told Ben.

'Where will you go?'

'I don't know. Back to the burrows.' She thought perhaps she would know how to be cruel. She had no regrets about the bounty hunter she had killed.

'I'll go with my father,' Ben said.

The three on the beach returned to share the fish.

'Hubert and I are going into the city,' Blossom said. 'We'll find the Limping Man and' – she hesitated – 'scrub all the evil out of his mind.'

'How?' Hana said.

Hubert said, 'We know how strong he is, but there are two of us. He might be able to hold one' – a look of pain crossed his face as he glanced at Blossom – 'but while he's busy the other will tie him in knots so tight he'll never get out.'

Ben fingered his knife. Dogshit, he thought.

Hana thought, They're children.

Blossom smiled at them. 'Can you think of any other way?'

'My father, what will you do?' Ben said.

'Sit still for a while,' Lo said.

'Will you go with them?'

'If I go I'll go by myself.'

'And take me with you?'

'No,' Lo said.

Before Ben could argue, Blossom hissed for silence.

'Men,' she said.

'How many?' Ben loosened his knife.

'A troop. A corporal. You can hear them now. They think this part of the forest is cleaned out.'

The sound of shouting came through the trees. It sounded like gulls fighting over scraps of food. Blossom and Hubert slipped away without a word.

'What are they doing?' Hana said.

'Throwing a rope around them,' Lo said.

'What sort of men?'

'Soldiers. City men. A crossbow troop.'

The sound of laughter stopped. A moment later Blossom and Hubert walked into the clearing, with a man in a doublet and cap walking in a dazed way between them. Blood Burrow, Hana thought. He seemed to see nothing.

'Where are the others?'

90

'Sleeping. This one is Foss. He'll tell us about the Limping Man.'

At the name, Foss lifted his hands and tried to make the straight and crooked sign. Blossom held him still.

'Who is this Limping Man?' she said.

'He's Lord. He's Master,' Foss said, making the sign this time.

'What does he do?'

'He leads us. He lifts us up. He gives us the world.'

'What world?' Hubert said.

'The forests. The plains. The seas to fish. But first we must clean the vermin out. Then the world is ours.'

'What are these vermin?'

'All who do not believe in him. All who do not love him.'

'How will you kill them?'

'With our armies. With our fleet.'

'Fleet?'

'We're building boats. They're ready to sail. They'll clean the coasts and burn the villages.'

'When?'

'Seven days.' He was fighting Blossom. He snarled at her. 'You witches will burn too. He'll make you scream.'

Blossom nodded. 'Sit down, Foss. Sleep a while.'

The man sat. His head slumped forward. He farted and snored.

'He'll follow this Limping Man till he dies,' Blossom said.

'It's like a stone in his head,' Hubert said.

'There's nothing else there.'

'Except his old cruelties slopping around like mud.'

'How will you stop the ships? You can't fight ships,' Ben said.

Blossom and Hubert looked at each other. They were uncertain. And, for all their courage, they were afraid.

91

'We'll go there. We'll find him,' Blossom said.

'Make sure you do it before they sail. Find out some more' – Ben kicked Foss – 'from this.'

Hubert woke Foss and questioned him about the size of the army. There were men from every tribe, Foss said, from the east, from the sea-coast and from the icelands in the south. Spearmen, bowmen, men armed with pikes and spears. There were squadrons of red horsemen armed with lances, and others with longbows that would shoot arrows over the moon. Lightly held, Foss mimed the shooting. Their leaders, he said, lived in tents outside the city. They worshipped the Limping Man each morning as the sun rose and each evening as it set. In eight days' time – Foss counted on his fingers – there would be a great burning of witches in People's Square, and a drowning of the men who consorted with them, and Dwellers too, vermin from the forests. Tears ran on Foss's cheeks as he thought of the pleasures he would miss. The following morning the army would march and the ships would sail.

'Tell us about these ships.'

'Four of them. Lovely ships. Sharp and fast and small. Ha, the sport they will have. Fifty bowmen on each one . . .' He wept again for his lost share of the pillage and the killing.

'Foss,' Blossom said, 'tell us how to get into the Limping Man's palace.'

Foss did not know. He was a burrows man. His job was to strengthen the garrison at Saltport. He told them that the ships were moored in the harbour at Port, that was all.

'Sleep, Foss,' Hubert said.

'And never wake up,' Hana whispered. This man might be one of those who had burned Mam.

Later in the morning Ben and Hana collected the weapons of the sleeping troop and threw them into a pool deep in the forest. They looked at the men snoring where they had fallen: burrows men and men from the half-emptied city of Ceebeedee. They looked peaceful, eyelids smooth, cheeks loose, yet several, mumbling, snarling, were having savage dreams. All wore the Limping Man's sign on their leather vests. One had the lines tattooed on the backs of his hands.

'Why don't I slit their throats?' Ben said.

'I'd sooner leave them sleeping here forever,' Hana said.

At the shelter Blossom and Hubert were ready to leave. Each carried a small pack and a knife in a sheath.

'What are you going to do, knock on his door?' Ben said.

They smiled distantly. It seemed to Hana they were already gone.

'Foss and his men will sleep until morning,' Blossom said. 'Be gone from here before they wake.' They made a small sign of farewell and slipped away like shadows, leaving silence round the shelter, until Foss snored. Ben banged the man's head with his heel to quieten him. He said to Lo: 'Where are we going, my father?'

They conversed silently, and Hana, concentrating, found she could hear them like voices in a neighbouring room.

I'm going where I was meant to go, Lo said.

Where? The city?

Into the forest, my son. To think a while.

To talk with the people?

If they'll hear me. My voice might not travel so far.

What will they tell you?

When I hear them I'll know. Go with the girl into the mountains.

That's not where she's going. And I'm coming with you.

Ben, you've given me great joy, Lo said. But I must go one way now and you another –

93

'No,' Ben said.

Lo rose from his seat by the ashes. He approached Ben and laid two fingers on his forehead.

We can never be apart, he said.

He turned away and slipped into the trees, more shadowy than Blossom and Hubert. He was gone before Ben could move.

Hana watched the boy. This, she thought, was like losing Mam. Ben moved one way, then the other. He did not seem to know where Lo had gone. Hana could not tell either but it did not surprise her that a man who was no longer a man should vanish like a shadow on a wall. It seemed to her he would find better ways of fighting the Limping Man than Blossom and Hubert would.

'Leave him,' she said.

'I want to go with him,' Ben whispered.

'He doesn't need you. You can come with me if you like.'

'Where?' Ben said. He seemed dazed. Each exit from the clearing was a way Lo might have gone.

'To the burrows,' she said. She smiled grimly at the thought: rubble, weeds, stinking mud, hovels made of rusty tin, puddles of foul water. She had no wish to go back. If she wanted to see Hawk again she would stay by the sea and on the hilltops. But Mam had died in the burrows. And the Limping Man was there.

She stuffed her blanket in her pack and fitted it on her shoulders.

'Are you coming?'

Ben grabbed his gear – his stone, his flint, his blanket. 'If you know the way.'

'I know it.'

'All right. Wait a minute.'

He was dazed with loss, but savage too and looking for

a way to restore himself. Hana made no move as he ran at Foss with his knife drawn. He put his foot on the man's out-stretched fingers and made a slash with the blade, then stabbed and sawed. He picked up Foss's severed thumb and threw it as hard as he could into the trees.

'That's what I'll do to the Limping Man. Let's go the quickest way we can.'

SEVEN

Patrols along the coast forced them inland. Ben saw that Hana had lost her way. She had no knowledge of the swamp lying between them and the city: brown reeds, sucking mud, pools with grey mist floating on their surface. Yelping frogs and booming toads deafened them. Swamp birds screamed. The dead water bubbled with reeking odours from deep down.

Ben found berry juice to smear on their skin. It kept mosquitoes from biting but not from swarming round their heads and blinding them. There were flies that drank from the corners of their eyes and leeches that fastened on their legs and sucked out blood. Ben showed Hana how to heat the tip of her knife and burn them off.

'There's the city,' Hana said.

Walls rose in the distance, over a plain beyond the swamp. They were like eroding cliffs and the buildings had jagged bites taken out of them. Only the hill, Company Hill, kept its shape: a hump-backed turtle smeared with grey-green trees. The red building rising in the midst was the Limping Man's palace. Hana, straining her eyes, made out its decoration of yellow flames.

There were tents around the city walls. She saw figures like black flies swarming among them.

'There's no way in.'

'We'll see,' Ben said. 'First we get across this swamp.'

'How?'

'Swim,' he said.

The pools at the fringes led to deeper ones. They sealed their packs and floated them, turning left and right through channels sometimes hooded with sedge. Mud islands stood in their way and they circled back. They slid on their bellies in shallow water and pulled themselves through rushes and over wet humps where flowers with the stink of corpses grew. Hana was not afraid. She had been in worse places in the burrows. She felt leeches fasten on her arms and legs. They would not kill her. Only men would kill her. She kept her limbs quiet in the water and her head low.

They reached the far edge of the swamp and eased their way into a fringe of rushes. Horsemen were wheeling in squadrons on the plain. Spare horses whinnied in corrals, where handlers groomed them. Tents stood in ordered rows with a man on guard outside each one. Even in the night there was no way for Ben and Hana to cross. They drew back, looking for another path. They would have to stay in the swamp, follow it inland and come to the city that way – or would it be better to find if it led down to the sea? Ben had taken charge. Hana let him. She had never been in this sort of place before.

'The sea,' he said.

They made their way back to the centre of the swamp, through humps of mud that gave them cover. At midday they opened their packs and drank from their bottles. Food could wait. They swam and slid towards the sea, drawn by its booming when the frogs fell silent.

Ben stopped suddenly, holding Hana still with his good arm.

'Island,' he whispered.

She slid alongside him.

'Someone living on it. I'll go and see.'

He left his pack and wriggled away. The island rose from a belt of reeds. A wooden shack, thatched with rushes, stood like a hooded eye. Ben circled to the far side, where the plain opened out, with horsemen drilling close by. A soldier guarded the entrance of a gravel causeway, lounging beside a pole with the Limping Man's pennant flapping in a breeze. Ben hated the symbol. The crooked line made him think of his lost hand.

A horseman cantered up. He handed the guard a canvas bag, waited while he looked in it, grinned at some joke and rode away. Flies swarmed round the bag. Food, Ben thought. He watched the guard saunter on the causeway, picking his way where water overlapped it. When he reached the island he tossed the bag towards the shack, yelling, 'Grub's up, Queenie. Come and get it.'

Sliding closer in the rushes, Ben saw the door move, heard it scrape. A grey-haired woman dressed in a belted shift scuttled out. She was bent like the handle of a shepherd's crook. Her hair, hanging loose, brushed the ground. She made clutching movements as she ran to the bag. She squatted by it, ferreted in it, then screamed like a disappointed gull: 'He's stolen it. He's eaten my cheese.'

The guard, halfway along the causeway, called over his shoulder: 'No cheese, Queenie. Cheese on odd days.'

'Stolen. My lovely cheese.' She rummaged again. 'Where's my eel?'

'Eels are in your head, Queenie. A bone is what you get. Dog bone and bread.'

'Thief. Liar. Oh my cheese! My eel! I'll tell your captain. I'll have you whipped.'

The guard made a two-fingered gesture over his shoulder and went on.

Ben watched as the woman gathered the bag in her arms and ran, crooked and crab-like, to her house. The door scraped shut and the swamp came back to life – yelping frogs, hooting toads. Ben slid back to Hana in the reeds.

'She's a prisoner.'

'Why aren't they burning her?' Hana said.

'I'm going to find out.'

They swam back to the forest and found a place to eat. Ben hunted for leaves to cool their leech bites. Then they slept in the shade for an hour.

'Now,' said Ben, waking.

'She'll call the guards.'

'Not when she sees what I've got.'

He followed a thin creek deeper into the forest, lay on the spongy ground, thrust his arm under a ledge and hauled out an eel. He pinned it under his foot and sliced off its head.

'She'll talk to us now.' He gutted the eel.

They crawled and swam back to the island. The scrub round the shack hid them from the soldiers on the plain. They went through scrawny trees, keeping low to the ground. Smoke drooped from a chimney, wrapping them. A canvas flap, waist high, covered an opening in the back wall. Ben gave Hana the eel. He scratched on the canvas.

'Queenie,' he whispered.

A screech, a scuttle, sounded inside. Then a voice like a cracked plate: 'Who is it? Who's there?'

'I've brought you something for your dinner.'

A hand pulled the canvas aside and the woman's head poked out. Hana had never seen an uglier face. It was broken-toothed and folded like bread-dough, with eyelids turned inside out. The eyes were alive though, quick and hungry.

'Where is it? What have you got?'

'An eel, Queenie. A fat one, see?' Ben took it from Hana and swung it in front of the woman. Her free hand snatched at it.

'Give it to me,' she screeched. 'I'll call my boy. My boy will make you.'

'Quiet, Queenie. The soldiers will hear. They won't let you have it. Where's your boy?'

'Everywhere. My boy's everywhere. You give it here.'

'Can we come in, Queenie? There's mosquitoes biting us. We'll help you cook it.'

'It's mine. You'll take it all.'

'No, it's for you. All yours.' He dangled the eel in front of her.

'Who's that with you? I don't like girls. They sneak things, girls.'

'She's my servant, Queenie. If she opens her mouth I'll give her a kick.'

'She can cook my eel. She can serve it to me. Have you got cheese?'

'No cheese, Queenie. The soldiers ate it. But here's your eel. Look how fat it is. You can have it all, we don't want any.'

She pulled the canvas aside. Ben handed the eel to Hana. He went into the shack, knife in hand. If she had a boy he would be waiting. Light from the window showed a table, a chair, an iron stove shaped like a pot, with a tin chimney rising through a hole in the roof. The bed was a wooden shelf piled with ragged blankets. Hana, coming through the flap, was reminded of the shelter she had shared with Mam.

The woman snatched the eel from her and hugged it to her breast.

'Eels is best. Eels is best,' she crooned.

Ben sheathed his knife. 'Why have they got you locked up, Queenie? What have you done?'

'I'm not locked up,' she said. 'This is my island. Ask my boy. But the soldiers steal my dinner. Have you come from him?'

'Who is your boy?' Hana said; and the woman shrieked at her, 'Girls don't talk. Girls keep their mouths shut. Make my bed, girl. Sweep my hearth.'

'Yes, girl, do it. Quick,' Ben said. He winked at her.

'I'll cook your eel if you like,' Hana said. 'But tell me first. Tell him.'

'Who needs telling?' said the woman. 'Everyone knows Vosper. Vosper is my boy. He grew up here, with me and his father, on this island. Vosper knows you're here. Vosper knows everything.'

'Where is Vosper?' Hana said. A cold idea was creeping in her.

'She's still talking, this girl. Hit her, boy. Make her kneel.'

'How did he hurt his leg?' Hana said.

'A kick, that's what he got. His father gave him a kick. It's what boys need. And plenty of good whippings. He saw to that. He had a lovely whip, made of horse-hide, Jug did. He whipped Vosper, it did him good. But he kicked him too hard. Bent his ankle like a tin spoon. Drowned soon after that, my poor Jug. Drowned in the swamp. Frogs and toads all over him.'

'And Vosper,' Hana said, 'he walks with a limp?'

'Limps, my boy. But he's good to me. He sends me meat. No one else gets meat. But they love him. Everybody does, even when there's nothing to eat. They look at my Vosper and they fall down on their knees.'

'The Limping Man,' Hana said to Ben.

He nodded. He looked pale.

'He's king of the world,' Queenie said. 'I'm the queen. Goat cheese, he sends me. But those soldiers bite it, I see their teeth. Cook my eel, girl, or I'll have you whipped.'

'No whipping, Queenie,' Ben said. 'Tell me how he makes people love him.'

'Ah,' she said, shaking her head, grinning sideways with her crumbled teeth, 'you've come for secrets. You want my secrets.'

'I'll bring you another eel,' Ben said.

'Eels is not enough. Not for secrets. There's people say he got too close to that poison salt. He sold frogs, my Vosper. They ate frogs, those Company. In silver dishes. Ottmar, King Ottmar, he ate frogs. Vosper went to the back door of them houses, frogs in his sack, hee hee, so they could eat the legs and lick their chops. The fat fools. The greasy chops. We wouldn't eat frogs, Jug and me, only toads eat frogs. But Vosper came home with silver pennies in his poke. We had more money than when Jug was alive.'

'Did he?' Hana whispered. 'Did he get too close to the poison salt?'

'Stories. All sorts of stories about him. Like he crawled out of the swamp or the forest or the sea. It's lies. I'm the one that knows. My Vosper is clever, he's so clever. He worked for that Clerk when he was king. He sniffed out things for that Clerk. But that was before.'

'Before what, Queenie?'

'She's talking. This girl is talking. Why haven't I got Jug's whip?'

'I'll cook your eel if you tell us,' Hana said. She reached for it and Queenie jerked away.

'I've got it. I got it from you. Ha!'

'Please tell us, Queenie,' Hana said.

The woman hugged the eel, sniffed it, licked the flesh where the head was severed.

Ben pulled Hana away. He hooked the stump of his arm over Queenie's shoulder and held his knife at her throat. 'Tell us,' he said.

She curled her mouth at him. Her eyes gleamed with cunning. 'Can't tell you if I'm dead, can I?'

He pricked her throat. A stain of red seeped into the folds of her skin. But she bared her brown teeth at him. 'Kill me, boy, and the toads will find out. There's no place you can hide from the toads.'

'Stop it, Ben,' Hana said.

'I can make her talk.'

'Stop it, I said.' She pulled his knife-arm away.

'Shouldn't let girls boss you. Bossy girls get burned,' Queenie said.

'Does he talk to them?' Hana said. 'Does Vosper talk to the toads?'

'Hear that, boy? Hear what she's doing? They sniff around. They find things out, girls do. But I don't tell. I never tell. I'm his ma but it wouldn't save me.'

'What do the toads say to him?' Hana whispered.

'No toads, girl. I never said toads.'

Hana stepped away. She was sorry for the old woman, frightened for her. She could see her chained to a stake in People's Square. But she had to know.

'How do you like your eels, Queenie? Boiled or baked?'

'Boiled is best, then there's soup. Don't touch it. And kneel down when you talk to me. If Vosper was here you'd kneel quick enough.'

'Right, I'm kneeling,' Hana said. 'Now, Queenie. Queen. Tell me the secret and I'll dig a hole for it, under the ground. Whisper to me.'

'Lower, girl. Kneel proper.'

Hana obeyed. 'I'll hide it where the toads will never know.'

Queenie, still hugging the eel, grinned at Ben. 'See how she thinks she can get what I know for nothing. Fair exchange is what you give for secrets. What have you got for Queenie? See their money first is what Jug said.'

'What happened to Vosper? How did he change?'

Queenie forgot her avarice. She smiled with pride. 'Ah, like tadpoles into frogs. He went out one day and he came home at night and put his hand right here.' She touched her forehead. '"Get down on your knees, Ma. Tell me how you love me." And I did. I got down. I cried out my eyes I loved my Vosper so hard. Light shone out of him.'

'How?' Hana whispered.

'And then he took his money and went down to the sea, past the burrows, where those traders come from the south, and he came home with cloth, finest cloth, it slides in your fingers, and he told me how to sew it, and I sewed. I made robes for him, red robes burning with yellow, and a red head-dress burning at the top, and he put them on and walked across the plain into the city and everyone fell down on their knees and worshipped him.'

'Why, Queenie. Why did they worship him?'

'I followed him but he turned and shouted, "Go back to your island, woman. Live on your island." And I did. I wait for him here. One day my Vosper will come.'

Tears streamed down her face. Hana stood up and took the old woman by the shoulders. She rocked her gently. 'He'll come, Queenie. But tell us how he changed. What did he do?'

Queenie drew back. She shook off Hana's hands. Her sad fallen cheeks bunched up, her eyes flashed with anger.

'Secrets. She wants my secrets. She'll try to hurt my Vosper, I can tell. Whip her, boy. Use your belt.'

Ben pushed Hana aside.

'What can I bring you, Queenie? Two eels? Two more fat ones? You can have them if you tell me instead of her. She'll never know. I'll climb up in the mountains and hide it in the snow. Then no one can ever hurt Vosper.'

Queenie's eyes darted. 'More than eels. I want more.'

'What then?'

'Cheese.'

'No cheese, Queenie. The soldiers have eaten it all.'

'Pigeons then. Bring me pigeons.'

'And then you'll tell?

'If they're fat ones. I haven't had a pigeon since Jug was drowned.'

'Two fat pigeons,' Ben said.

'Plucked and gutted.'

'All right. Tomorrow. In the morning. But no pigeons if you don't tell me. You'll have to live off dog bones till you die. Now cook your eel.'

He lifted the canvas flap. 'Come on, girl. Hurry up or you'll get a kick.'

Hana stooped through the flap. He pushed her with his foot.

'Tomorrow, Queenie. Fair exchange.'

'Plucked and gutted,' the woman said. 'And mind they're fat. So I can push my finger in. This eel's not fat.'

'It's good enough. Tomorrow, eh? I've got to go and give this girl a whipping.'

'Hit her hard. Make her cry.'

They stooped through the bushes at the back of the island, waded into the water and swam to the forest. Before leaving the swamp Ben cut several flax leaves and wrapped them round his waist.

'If you kick me tomorrow I'll kick you,' Hana said. 'Where it hurts.'

'Just doing it for Queenie,' Ben said.

They found a place to rest in the trees. Ben scraped the flax leaves and tied three snares.

'Why three?'

'One for us. I'm getting hungry.'

He vanished into the trees. Hana found a stream and washed the mud smell off her body and out of her clothes. It would be back tomorrow but her mind felt muddy too, after the woman. She found a place where the sun broke through the canopy and put her clothes on bushes to dry. What could Queenie tell them? Some spell the Limping Man spoke? Some magic sign he made? Hana did not believe it. Mam had said there was no magic, everything was natural and could be understood. Some food he ate, then, or mixture he drank? Wasn't that magic too in its way? There was something though, and magic or not it came from the toads. Did he slide down into the swamp with them the way she climbed her silver rope to Hawk in the sky? Did he find his strength there? If she knew then maybe she and Ben could find a way to strip it away. Queenie had said he could be hurt.

She lay down in the sun by the stream. How did a thin weak boy, whipped and crippled by his father, turn into the Limping Man? She felt sick with the thought of him – how he had suffered, what he had become. She had no doubt that somehow he had drowned his father.

After a while she slept, dreaming in fragments that chipped and dug in her mind before sliding away: the Limping Man, the drowned men in People's Square, Queenie with yellow teeth that wanted to bite, and Hawk at last, Hawk circling in the blue, with Mam on a hillside watching him.

When she woke Ben was sitting beside her.

'You've been crying,' he said. He flicked a tear off her cheek.

'It's none of your business,' she said. She wiped her face.

'You better put your clothes on or I'll think you're one of those Bawdhouse doxies.'

She had never heard the word but understood what it meant.

'I washed myself and you stink, so why don't you do it too?' She jumped up and grabbed her clothes and pulled them on while he watched, grinning.

'I set my snares.'

'You can keep your pigeons.' She went back to the camp, where she ate strips of dried fish and drank water. A baked pigeon, she thought. It was what she wanted more than anything in the world.

That night before sleeping they talked about Queenie and her secret, but neither could work out what it might be, and neither was sure it would defeat the Limping Man.

'It might be something we can tell Blossom and Hubert,' Hana said.

'If we can find them. But I'll tell you what,' Ben said, 'if I meet the Limping Man I'll call him Vosper.'

Hana shook her head. To her that hissing name did not make the Limping Man smaller, it made him worse.

They passed the night uneasily, waking at every noise. Ben checked his snares at dawn and came back with three pigeons. He cleaned them while Hana lit a small fire. He packed one of the pigeons with mud and they left it in the embers while they scouted the edge of the swamp. The same soldier was guarding the entrance to the causeway. As they watched, smoke rose from Queenie's chimney.

'She's warming up her soup,' Ben said.

Back at their camp, they peeled off the mud and ate the

pigeon. It tasted of berries. They put out the fire, hid their packs in the trees, and went back to the swamp. Smoke still came from Queenie's chimney. It slumped in the heavy air, making a brown cap on the island. The guard was at his post and crossbowmen were shooting at wooden targets on the plain. The thud of their bolts carried across the swamp.

'Something's wrong,' Ben said.

'What?'

'I can't hear any frogs.'

They listened. Only the faint hiss of gas escaping in the swamp.

'Why's the guard standing like that?' Yesterday he had lounged. Today he stood wide-legged, half at ease, half at attention, with his spear held across his chest.

'Someone's watching him.'

'Who?'

'Hidden somewhere. I'm going to see.'

'No, Ben. They'll be on the island.'

'They won't see me, I'll see them first. If I can get in I can talk to her. Give me the pigeons.'

He tied a flax thread through their gullets and hung the birds on his chest.

'Get out of here, Hana. Get the packs and head down to the coast. Keep away from the swamp. I'll meet you where it drains into the sea.'

She remembered a brown stream trickling from the sandhills. It seemed to flow in another time.

'They'll catch you,' she said.

'Not me. Hana, we've got to find out what she knows.'

He chose an arm of the swamp hidden from the island, slipped into the water, eased his way to a wider reach and sank. Hana lay watching in the trees. She would go when she knew he was safe. From time to time he surfaced behind a

108

clump of rushes. He was like a swamp creature, rising and sinking without a ripple or sound.

Half the morning was gone. There was no sign of Queenie. The frogs were silent but a toad boomed here and there. She searched the piece of sky she could see. No dot against the blue. Hawk too was in another time.

Ben's head rose, black and sleek. He faced the long stretch at the back of the island. She felt him take a deep easy breath and submerge . . .

Everything was done by touch – fingers reading the slope of the mud and the deep knots of fibrous root. His stump felt things out as well as his hand. Memory and his sense of distance were a tool. Queenie's island while his breath lasted. Another clawed grip in the mud, another slow frog-kick – he was there. He eased to the surface. Nothing but rushes, a wall of them that would hiss and bend and give him away if he tried to pass. He crept sideways under water and rose again. The way was clear along a tongue of mud and through the bushes to the canvas door at the back of Queenie's shack.

He half rose, peered about, gripped his knife – and heard Hana's scream from across the water. A man stepped from the bushes and loosed a crossbow bolt but Ben had already thrown himself to one side. Others were bursting from the scrub. Without a pause he threw himself again. Bolts pocked the water. One scorched a groove along his thigh; but he was under and heading deep as the men plunged in. Where would they expect him to go? Away from the island, aiming for the forest over the swamp. Some would be re-arming for a second shot.

He swam hard along the bottom until he had used half his time. Then he released a breath of air – a signal to his hunters that he was heading where they expected. They would watch for him where the bottom shelved into drowned reeds a quarter way across. Ben turned and headed back for the island, angling to avoid men surging out chest deep. Spearmen, he guessed. They would probe for him. The water stirred along his side as one went past. Ben kept swimming softly – his good arm, his stump, his legs in unison. He reached a patch of reeds beyond the mud-hump where he had landed and lay on his back, with only his face showing. He breathed deep and quiet, then sank again. For the next hour he worked his way round the island. Once, shielded by reeds on every side, he watched soldiers struggling through the water. A bowman lost his footing and went under. He came up, went under again and no one tried to save him. His last cry was, 'Praise the Man.' The next time Ben looked boats were rowing in the deep parts of the swamp and men stabbed the water with spears. Others had landed in the forest but Ben was confident Hana was away. They would not catch her in the trees.

A small man dressed in black and thin as a stick shrilled orders from the largest boat. Ben could not make out his words but saw him point: he wanted the reeds round the island searched. There was no hope now of slipping through the bushes to Queenie's shack. Ben cut the pigeons free from his neck and wedged them in roots under the surface. He worked his way further round the island until he felt the gritty rise of the causeway. Nowhere to go. He changed direction, heading deeper into the fringe of reeds. An eel writhed away under his chest. He scraped along the bottom until his breath gave out. Something – a log? – stopped him from surfacing. He felt a hand clamp his head, and fought his terror – not a hand, a piece of heavy cloth. He tore it away, raised his face in the water, and looked into Queenie's dead eyes.

Blood had drawn eels like perfume. They twisted round

the body, wrapping Queenie in their arms. Ben drew deep breaths, calming himself. He felt for a wound and found three crossbow bolts embedded in her chest. It meant she had not been killed trying to run. They had made her talk and she had told about a boy and girl and their questions . . .

The sound of oars closed in. There was no hiding place. Ben held his knife tight. What would Hari do? What would his father? It was Lo's voice he seemed to hear: Use what is there. But there was nothing: reeds, mud, water. There was only his knife. *Use what is there.* Eels, a body. His mind made a kick. It was as though he had become Lo.

Ben slid under Queenie's body, pushing eels out of the way. He surfaced in the gap between her and the reeds. The shouting of men, the sound of oars, came closer. He chose a reed, cut it below the water and snapped off its top. He blew through the hollow stem, making sure it was clear. Then he slid under Queenie, his head beneath hers where it butted into the reeds. He thrust the reed upwards through her hair, blew it free of water and started to breathe. It was hard. For a moment he thought he would not get enough air. He changed to shallow breaths, using the top of his lungs. He could last that way if the boats were quick. He felt one bump Queenie's body. Her hair drifted, circling his throat. Eels thrashed away. Ben imagined he heard shouts and wondered if he was blacking out. He held on. There *was* enough air. Lo, he thought, I believe in you.

An oar scraped his side as the boat backed out of the reeds. Ben waited. One minute. Two. They were still close. He felt water shift as spearmen trod in the rushes by the shore. Then the movements stopped. Only the eels moved. He felt them nibbling the wound in his thigh.

Slowly he let his face rise through Queenie's hair. Blue sky, a reed wall, half her face, one eye. He drew a proper breath and sank again. The next time he lifted his head high enough to listen. The shouts and the treading had moved towards the back of the island. One boat was still close. He heard the swish of a spear plunged into water. They were not giving up. He heard the little man shriek orders – a voice like a girl's, a voice like Hana's, who had saved him.

Ben sank again. He stabbed at the nibbling eels with his knife – and all afternoon he kept it up, rising, breathing, sinking, repulsing the eels. Queenie's body wanted to float away. He took a handful of her hair and pulled it back each time. The sun edged down the western sky – taking its time. When night came he would move, swim silently down the length of the swamp to the place where it drained into the sea. Until then he must lie alongside his companion.

'What's the secret, Queenie?' he whispered.

He wondered if the Limping Man had ordered his mother's death.

Feet tramped on the causeway and died away. After a while frogs began to croak. Toads boomed. The sun sank slowly. Lazy bloody sun, Ben thought. He waited an hour after it was dark. There was no sound on the island – no twig snapping, no shuffle or step round Queenie's shack.

Ben whispered goodbye to the old woman. Quietly he made his way out into the swamp.

EIGHT

A trickle of water ran through beds of yellow grass. Hana waited where it broke out on the beach, hugging the packs to stay warm. After screaming her warning she had run. Ben was alive, she was sure of it. He was so quick, so confident, so easily a part of every place he found himself in that she believed he would simply sink into the swamp and vanish like a frog.

She waited while the sun went down, hearing waves rustle on the sand. Stars came out and she named them, as Danatok had taught her. But always she was listening, listening for Ben. She kept her mind open for him the way she had for Hawk. Speaking, she thought. Maybe we should speak. Several times in the last few days she had caught whispers from him. Perhaps he heard her too. Perhaps it was natural between them. If she said his name now alongside her own, made a link between them, he might find his way to her as if she were a light for him to see. But she hesitated. She did not like people in her mind and nor did he. He spoke with Lo, and she, in some strange way, had spoken with Hawk. It was enough. Speaking with Ben would be like letting him put his hand on her. She was not ready for that.

She wrapped herself in her blanket. She counted stars – and opened her mind for him when she remembered, without speaking his name. She would be a place for him to find but not a voice calling.

The wind rose and waves beat louder on the beach. Where was he? It must be midnight. She began to imagine him pierced with crossbow bolts, floating dead in the rushes with eels like black banners hanging from his chest and belly.

Ben, she said at last, where are you?

Another hour passed. She counted time by the movement of the earth, the way Danatok had taught her. The swamp was moving too, with night creatures, bubbling gas, and its own stillness, which was like an explosion clamped down by a lid of mud and water.

'Ben,' she whispered. The waves answered. The wind answered. A night bird, on the wing, answered with a distant cry.

Ben, she thought.

He replied. It was like a hand touching and falling away. Hana, he said, and nothing more. She held on to the sound. She imagined a thread running through the dark and she slid her hand along it, followed it. The way led up the creek trickling in the sand, then into the swamp grass and towards the forest.

Ben, she said again, and he replied, stronger now: Hana.

She followed the shred of warmth that came from him, and found him where the reeds began. He was no more than a shine of eyes in the starlight; then a shine of teeth – he was trying to grin.

'Wondered when you'd get here,' he said in a voice she scarcely heard.

'Ben, are you hurt?'

114

'In my leg. Flies, mosquitoes, bloody eels. Bloody toads. Everything's biting me. I'm the best dinner they've ever had.'

She felt his exhaustion. 'Don't talk.'

Stumbling, sinking, she helped him along the swamp-edge, through the rank grass, down to the beach. She wrapped his blanket round him but would not let him lie down.

'We've got to move, Ben. They'll be hunting us in the morning.'

'Send them the wrong way,' he whispered.

She had already thought of it. She left him by the stream and walked along the beach, leaving footprints where the high tide would not wash them away. Then she angled down to the sea, still heading north, went into the water up to her knees and turned back to the stream. She walked up until she found Ben. He was sleeping. She woke him, helped him stand and shuffle to the stream; left him swaying there while she scuffed out his marks in the sand, hoping she had them all. She meant the searchers to think Ben had died in the swamp.

Together, Hana supporting Ben, they waded down the stream into the sea.

'Where are we going?' he mumbled.

'I know a place.'

The sea water seemed to revive him. He took his pack from her and stuffed his blanket in, then drank water from his bottle. 'I'm full of mud,' he said; and was at once sick into the sea. He drank again.

'Come on, Ben. We've only got a couple of hours,' she said.

'One good thing, the salt water gets rid of the leeches.'

Knee-deep, sometimes shoulder-deep in the waves, she led him to the tumbled rocks at the foot of the cliffs. Up there, the Limping Man was sleeping in his palace. And over the hill lay the ruins of the city that had been Belong. I'm going back to the burrows, Hana thought. It almost made her sick like Ben. She was sick with fear.

They found the cave she had hidden in on her flight from the burrows. The sun came up, lighting its mouth as they went inside. She led Ben round two curves into the dark and found a place for them to lie on a fan of sand. They slept all day, refilled their bottles from the water trickling down the wall, and crept out as night swept down like a black fog. Ben found seaweed and bound it with strips of blanket to the cut in his thigh. Hana heard him grunting with pain but dared not show sympathy. They had to keep moving.

Halfway through the night they took to the sea. Hana had no knowledge of the sea wall, just a memory of Danatok's tale of his house on stilts. She found the gap into the harbour and they peered through. Fires were burning on the road running behind the wharves. Men moved back and forth loading ships. This was the fleet Foss had boasted of: four single-masted vessels with oars along their sides and bows like beak-fish. It was hard to tell in the night, but they seemed to have the limping symbol painted on their sides.

Ben and Hana swam silently, keeping clear of the firelight on the water. The stilt house made a shadow and they moved along it like a road. A wall had fallen outwards, giving shelter as they drew close.

'Ben,' Hana whispered.

'Yeah,' he replied. He freed his pack, pushed it at her, sank without a sound. I seem to spend half my life under water, he thought. He came up beside a pile crusted with shellfish and sent his mind into the room above, probing in corners and feeling along walls. He beckoned Hana.

The fallen wall made a stairway hiding them from the shore. They climbed and found an open room, grey in the dawnlight. The built-in bunks and iron stove were torn from their places and made a rubble heap on the floor, where rotten planks gave glimpses of the water below. No one would use the pile house again. No one would come.

They drank from their bottles but had no food left. Ben made a sack of his shirt. He climbed down the sloping wall and filled it with mussels from the piles. They opened them with their knives and ate them raw. Then they slept uncomfortably, disturbed by the shouts of men and the rumble of carts from the wharves.

The sun was high when they woke. A wind was blowing from the east, rattling loose timbers on Danatok's house. Hana and Ben were trapped until dark. Even then they had no idea where they would go. She helped him untie the bandage on his thigh. The wound was clean, but although he was stoical she saw how it hurt him. The leech bites and insect bites troubled him with their itching. He needed to head back to the forest for cool leaves and healing berry juice. Hana counted the days they had spent: four days gone, two to go before the burnings in People's Square. The army would march the day after that. And these four deadly ships were almost ready to sail. She felt helpless. What could they do, two of them against the Limping Man? And where were Blossom and Hubert? Where was Lo? She sat with her back to a wall and let Ben watch the shore through a crack between two twisted planks. He did not seem to have these questions. Every now and then he drew his stone out of his pocket and worked on the edge of his knife.

She was dozing when she felt his hand on her shoulder. At once she knew something had changed. The wind still rattled the house but a hush lay under it. His hand took her shirt and hauled her up. She put her eye to the crack. The workers stood still, the carts had stopped. Even the horses watched as two people, side by side, walked along the empty road towards the wharf where the ships were moored. They did not hurry, they looked as if they were strolling on a path: Blossom and Hubert.

'Don't,' Hana said as she felt Ben's mind crouch and prepare to spring. 'They don't need us. If they know we're here we'll get in the way.'

She saw their concentration and unity. Each was held in the other's hand – Hana felt it the way she had felt Hawk. They moved as easily as he flew yet she felt the strength hidden by their ease, like tree roots anchored on stone.

'I want to help them,' Ben said.

'You can't.'

A squad of bowmen ran along the wharf. The line in front knelt to shoot, the line behind stood ready.

Blossom and Hubert 'spoke' a command. Hana felt it ripple across her mind: heard a sound like the small hiss of a wave at its furthest reach on the sand. The bowmen laid down their weapons and made no other move as Blossom and Hubert passed through their lines. The workers and their overseers stepped back as though an unseen hand was pushing them. Their arms fell slack at their sides. Blossom and Hubert turned to the ships. Another command. The men on board trooped off and stood with the others.

'The Limping Man must know. He must feel it by now,' Ben said.

Hana feared this too. But his palace was miles away on the hill. She wondered why Blossom and Hubert had not gone there to challenge him. Then she understood. Piles of hay lay on the wharf to feed the cart-horses. Men began to carry armfuls up the gangplanks and drop them in the holds of the ships. Blossom and Hubert waited. Hana felt the strength of their concentration: more than a hundred men in control. If one broke out all would follow. They would fall on Blossom and Hubert and tear them to pieces like a dog pack with a pair of trapped hares.

Four men bound hay to lengths of wood. Another with a flint and stone struck sparks on the hay. Four torches flamed. The men walked one to each ship. They mounted the gangplanks and stood by the open holds. Again Hana felt the ripple of Blossom and Hubert's command. The men threw their torches, which plunged red and eager into the bellies of the ships, each with a tail of smoke behind it.

It took only a moment. White smoke first, swaying and curling. Then puffs of flame, tongues of flame, leaping tigers of flame. Red fire climbed out of the holds and ran on the decks. It climbed the masts and ate the furled sails. It bent over the sides of the ships, caressing them and hissing on the water.

The men on the wharf took no notice, although the nearest ones beat out sparks eating their clothes. Blossom and Hubert stood as though unaware of the roaring furnaces by the wharf. They disappeared and reappeared behind walls of flame. They stood as though waiting and – Hana was uncertain in the haze of heat and the slanting flames – now each had an arm around the other's waist.

'Why aren't they getting away?' she said.

The fires lost their anger, they settled down to burn steadily. Soon they would eat through the hulls. Then the ships would go down one by one. Ben's throat was swelling, his eyes were burning with joy and anticipation.

'They're waiting for Vosper,' he said. 'They'll burn him up the way they're burning the ships.'

Distantly, above the noise of the fire, they heard a trumpet cry.

'He's on his way. I'm going to help them.' He stepped away from the crack.

'No, Ben. You'll get in the way. Can't you feel' – she could not describe it – 'feel the way they're aimed like a spear. They'll break if they have to think about anyone else.' It was true, she felt it – their strength, so concentrated, was also delicate. She wanted to see their faces. Their faces would glow.

At a new command the workers and bowmen turned like sleepwalkers and shuffled into the streets leading from the wharves. They vanished among the buildings, leaving the carts and horses, leaving their weapons strewn on the ground. The ships continued to burn, flaring, subsiding, crackling with small explosions as timbers parted in the flames. A mast fell hissing into the sea, and as it fell the trumpet blared again.

'The Limping Man,' Hana whispered.

'Vosper,' Ben said. He dug his knife into the wall.

Blossom and Hubert were tiny on the wharf. Suddenly they looked frail. Hana wished for Hawk's eyes to see them better. Danatok had told her about the great voice gifted speakers heard – Pearl and Hari had heard it saying their names, joining them to the spirit animating the world. Xantee had heard it. Blossom and Hubert too. They heard it now, making them ready. Hana was sure of it, although until now she had believed it was nonsense. She seemed to hear a whisper, an edge of sound. Taste it too. It tasted like honey.

Ben said, awestruck: 'They're hearing something, aren't they?'

'The voice,' Hana whispered.

Then he shivered. And Hana, her eyes drawn away from the twins, shivered too. At the far end of the wharf, where it began its run along the waterfront, a man dressed in black appeared from one of the dark streets. He carried a naked sword that lit up in the sun and a trumpet slung around his neck. Behind him came four bearers, stolid and in step, carrying a litter enclosed in walls of cloth that rippled like fire. Yellow flames within the red darted and licked. Two small men, black-clad like the trumpeter and as thin as wire, walked with prancing steps beside the litter. That was all. There were none of the guards and constables Hana had seen in People's Square. The Limping Man needed no one but himself.

'Vosper,' Ben said. 'I want to see him.'

'You will,' Hana said. She was sick with dread. Blossom and Hubert, in their forest clothes, looked weak and puny. She wondered if they still heard the voice. She could not. And she knew with a certainty that pierced her like a knife, that the Limping Man heard a voice too – the *other* one.

'Ben, he'll kill them.'

'No he won't. Look at the ships, Hana. They did that.'

The vessel at the head of the line was sinking stern first. It went down slowly, with water swelling from its hold as though from a spring. At the end of the line the fourth one was turning on its side. Explosions of steam shot out as the water reached the seat of the fire. The two in the centre were hooded in red flames and brown smoke.

The ships were destroyed, the Dweller villages were safe, Stone Creek was safe. But Hana knew it was only a little part. It was like kicking a snapping dog out of the way. The multitude of tents on the plains remained, the armies remained. And the Limping Man, who held their ten thousand minds cupped in his hands, was here on the wharf. He was unchanged.

The crier raised his trumpet and blew another blast. It rasped like a saw. Hana put her hands over her ears, but Blossom and Hubert did not seem to hear. They were like two plants growing side by side and intertwining. The crier, the attendants, the bearers were people. They seemed to creep and hop and strut and not feel the air surrounding them. They're underground people, Hana thought. He's buried them.

The bearers set the litter down and stepped away. The attendants drew the curtains aside. The crier was ready, saluting with his sword. He raised his face to the sky and bellowed, 'See the Man. Worship him.' The attendants knelt, while the bearers lay face down on the wharf.

Blossom and Hubert smiled. Across the water, Hana felt their challenge rather than saw it. It was like the morning light rising into the dark. It was like the first glow of the sun. But she felt a dreadful hollowness inside. The dark always swallowed the light. Night came in the end, it always came.

'Morning too,' she whispered. 'Morning comes.'

'What?' Ben said.

She could not say what she meant, she could only watch. The Limping Man's stick prodded out of the litter. He followed, stepping down in his painful way. Red robes, yellow flames, tall head-dress: he was the same. She could not see his face through the smoke but had an impression of whiteness and pinkness, of a weak-eyed face, of a trembling body inside the garish robes. It was a lie. She had seen in People's Square how strong he was. Her own body trembled with fear.

He put his weight on his stick. He limped past the prostrate bearers and the kneeling attendants. The crier rose to his feet. He seemed the powerful one, yet he writhed to a shorter stature as he came to the Limping Man's side. The Limping Man whispered. The crier listened. Along the wharf, a ship's length away, Blossom and Hubert waited.

The crier raised himself to his full height. He lifted his sword over his head.

'Listen,' he cried. His voice was like a cracking whip. It seemed he could wrap it around Blossom and Hubert and haul them in. 'Listen to the voice of the Limping Man. Bow down to the Limping Man. Worship him.'

Blossom and Hubert shook their heads slightly, as though some night creature had brushed by and left its odour. They ignored the crier. They spoke silently to the Limping Man. Hana and Ben saw him start and lean convulsively on his stick. The twins' voice was easy. Ben and Hana heard it too, touching their minds.

There is no worship of people, Blossom and Hubert said.

The crier shrank again to hear the Limping Man's instructions. Then, at his full height, he bellowed, 'These vermin of the forests invade our city. Listen all, listen my subjects, you in the streets, come forth and listen. They have sunk my ships. It does not matter. I will build better ones. And I will punish these creatures that slink from the forests. See the man. I will drown him. See the woman. She will burn.'

'Who's he talking to?' Hana whispered.

'Look,' Ben said.

The ruined streets beyond the wharves were like caves in a cliff face. Slowly, in ones and twos, people began to creep out. They stopped, they fell back, they started again, as Hubert and Blossom on one side and the Limping Man on the other, fought for control of them. It was, Hana felt, like the sun rising, while the night, shaped like a hand, wrapped its fingers round it and tried to crush its light. Blossom and Hubert said: He is nothing. Free yourselves. The people they had sent away, the wharfmen and cartmen and soldiers, crept out: painful steps, pushing against a huge weight. They crept out.

Come, my people, worship me, said the Limping Man.

'He's winning,' Hana said.

'He's stronger,' Ben said, sliding his knife in and out of its sheath.

The men from the shadows came steadily, like a tide. They rolled across the empty wharf, brown and black and red and white, with their eyes burning and teeth flashing. The bowmen picked up their weapons. The cartmen and sailors fumbled in their belts and drew their knives. Blossom and Hubert fought. They tightened their unity, gripped each other hard, with minds that had learned to jump over mountains and seas and throw knowledge back and forth like balls in a game – and it was not enough. They could not hold the creeping tide. All their strength went into the effort. They had none for the Limping Man.

He struck. There was nothing to see, but Hana was aware of a shadow, a force. It jumped over the heads of the advancing men and landed on Blossom and Hubert like a toad, flinging them apart, throwing them backwards. Their agonised mouths howled at the sky. Then there was nothing to see except their bodies crumpled on the wharf.

Ben gave a cry of anguish. Hana doubled up with pain.

The men surged, with weapons raised and mouths jabbering. They looked as if they meant to tear Blossom and Hubert with their teeth. Shriller than their noise came a piping cry: 'Stop.' It was the Limping Man speaking with his own voice. The crier followed with a monstrous bellow: 'Stop.' The men stood frozen over Blossom and Hubert, with knives raised and teeth bared.

The crier stooped. The Limping Man whispered.

'Do you think you can act for yourselves?' the crier bellowed. 'Have I told you to slay the vermin? Leave them. They are mine. The woman will burn. The man will drown. And you who forget me and act for yourselves, you will worship me. Now. Down on your knees to the Limping Man.'

The crowd obeyed, some weeping, others shouting their love.

'That is what I require from you. Obedience. Is there a soldier who will die for me?'

Men sprang to their feet and ran forward. The crier put his hand on one and motioned the others back. The Limping Man raised his stick and beckoned. He whispered to the chosen man, who knelt and placed his forehead on the ground. Then he sprang up – a young man, full of strength – ran to the nearest ship and jumped with a cry into the burning hold.

A single exhalation, a unified breath of satisfaction: no other sound on the wharf until the crier, in a lowered voice, said, 'That is the love I require.'

The Limping Man turned away. He stepped into the litter painfully, his head stooping, his red and yellow robes curling round his flanks. He drew in his stick. The attendants stepped forward to pull the curtains closed. His pale hand stopped them as the crier knelt. One of the burning ships broke in half. Its bow and stern rose in the air, shedding water. The men around Blossom and Hubert swayed and moaned. Several ran at the twins with bared knives.

'Hold,' the crier bellowed. 'They belong to me, to the Limping Man. You will have your revenge in People's Square. Go to your homes now. Worship me and I will give you all you desire. I will build these ships again. You will rule the seas. My armies will march. The plains, the forests, the mountains will be yours if you obey me. Go now. Assemble in two days' time in People's Square and you will see the man drown and the woman burn. Fetch a cart for them – you and you. The rest, go to your homes while my patience lasts.'

The soldiers drifted away in no order. The workers melted into the dark streets. The cartmen took their horses and plodded along the wharf, except for one and his helper, who stopped beside the bodies of Blossom and Hubert. They took them by the arms and legs and flung them in the cart.

The attendants closed the litter curtains. With the crier marching in front, blowing trumpet blasts, the attendants prancing and the bearers in step, the Limping Man left the wharf. His red litter withdrew like a tongue into a mouth. The cart followed, with Blossom and Hubert motionless in the tray.

Beside the wharf the last of the burning ships rolled on its side.

NINE

Hana and Ben slept curled up in opposite corners of the room. Grief was like a drug, shutting them down.

When Ben woke he climbed down the broken wall for shellfish. Hana opened her eyes to find him eating. He pushed mussels towards her with his foot.

'I never thought they'd beat him,' he said.

'Nor did I,' Hana whispered.

'He's too strong. So . . .' He cut a mussel hinge and flicked the shell open. 'That's the only way to deal with Vosper.'

'Ben, you'll never get close.'

He swallowed the mussel. 'I can try. What are you going to do?'

'I don't know. But Queenie would have told us –'

'Queenie's dead.'

'So will you be if you try to fight him. What we've got to do is find out.'

They argued. Ben was angry and aggressive and Hana stubborn. Although he was afraid, he trusted himself. If he could get close to the Limping Man and make one throw . . . Hana did not believe he would ever get close, and if he did, by some piece of luck, the man had defences that would freeze Ben's arm. Hers was the only way that had a chance. She wanted to watch him. She wanted to find the secret Queenie knew. What then? Then Ben could throw his knife through the hole she made.

They waited for dark. Across the water the half-sunken ships steamed and flickered. Now and then people came out of the streets to watch but soon drifted away. A haze of smoke lay over the harbour. The sun turned red as it sank towards the horizon. Somehow it reminded Hana of Lo – its quietness, its sinking. She did not believe any help would come from Lo. When Ben thought of him he brooded on what he felt was his father's failure to trust him. He was also troubled by the fear that Lo had deserted, Lo had gone back to the people.

Dark came quickly. It was too dangerous to go into the streets of Port. They drank the last of their water and tied the empty bottles round their necks. Belting on their knives, they swam quietly to the sea wall and moved along its seaward side. One thing they agreed on, the Limping Man was in his palace. They would go there.

The wall ended. They climbed among the rocks below the cliffs. A thin moon was rising over the mountains. They found the cave they had slept in and filled their water bottles and went on. It was past midnight when they reached the beach. A steep hill, part cliff, rose on their right. That, guarded or not, was their way. They 'spoke' clumsily, bouncing and skidding in each other's heads.

No guards.

No.

The moon threw a pale light, barely enough for them to make out the shapes of trees. They darted from one to the next.

Cliffs.

Can you do it?

She meant, can you climb with only one hand?

He hissed at her angrily. And she was surprised at how nimbly he climbed. By now she should have known what he could do. He used his shortened arm as a lever. He swung his legs sideways and hooked his toes into cracks in the rock wall.

There was a guard at the top. His mind was sleepy. He yawned. He stopped to piss against a rock. The splashing hid the rustle of their feet as they darted into the trees. Again they used their minds, feeling ahead. The gift was new to them, they used it together, helping each other as they moved through scrub along the clifftop. Close to the edge, a squat shape rose in the dark: a building, unguarded.

Ben, it's the place Danatok told me about. Where the Limping Man feeds his toads.

Empty now.

The door was half open, creaking in the breeze that stirred the trees. They peered inside. In the back wall, over the cliff, was the window where Danatok had spied. Moonlight, pale as water, slanted in the door, showing empty tanks and cages.

He doesn't use it any more.

Guard coming, Ben said.

They darted inside. Ben slid out his knife.

The man tramped along one side of the building, then the other. He stood at the edge of the cliff. They heard him rattling shell nuts in his pocket and cracking them. They heard him chewing. He came back, stopped at the door and banged it with the heel of his spear.

'Man, help me prosper,' he muttered, then trudged away.

Ben sheathed his knife. They waited a moment, then slipped into the trees.

'You can tell Vosper grew up in a swamp,' Ben whispered. 'Keeping toads.'

Quiet, Ben. Speak, don't talk, Hana said.

They crept from tree to tree. Soon they came to a stone smothered in scrub, with parts rising above the foliage. It was a moment before they understood: this was the hand, carved from marble in the days when Company had ruled. The horizontal stone, lying over the bushes, was a finger pointing west to the land where Company began – where the armies that conquered Belong and the ships that carried them had gathered. The raised stone, shaped like a tree stump, was a thumb. A few paces further on, through wiry scrub, was the place where Hari and Pearl had taken each other by the hand and jumped into the sea. Ottmar's mansion had stood further back, set in a park. In a later time, Xantee had fought the mother gool deep in a basement under the ruins. And somewhere close, the Limping Man had built his palace. Ben climbed to the base of the thumb, but saw only scrub stretching away. Hana stepped on to the broken tip of the finger, where it lay half buried in low bushes. She turned her head from the edge of the cliff and the dizzy fall into the sea. The moon over the mountains, the water shining with its borrowed light, seemed to make another kind of darkness. Deep pits of shadow lay everywhere. A line of black trees rose beyond the scrub. The palace must be on the other side.

They climbed down silently. Hana followed Ben as he wriggled through the scrub. He was as slippery as a snake. She tried to copy him, using her own skills of moving through broken streets and climbing over rubble without stirring a stone.

Slower, Ben.

They passed through the jagged trees. The ground was damp on the other side. Head-high ferns grew in place of the scrub. They came across slabs of marble in the shape of shells: a ruined fountain, dry inside.

Ben stopped.

Lawn, he said.

Hana did not know what a lawn was. But she knew the thing rising beyond the flattened grass: unlit, low – the Limping Man's palace.

Guard, Ben said.

They lay still. The man slouched along the back of the building. He reached the corner and waited until a second man appeared behind him. They saluted each other, their leather jerkins gleaming in the moonlight. Then the first man went from sight while the other tramped in his place along the rear side.

They go round and round. There'll be four, Ben said.

There's no windows or doors, Hana said.

There's a door somewhere, unless he can fly.

They backed away from the fountain and went along the line of trees until it curved towards the sea. Scrub, thicker than before, covered everything. Ben had to cut branches and push them aside as he crawled. They came across the ruins of a mansion – perhaps, Hana thought, House Bowles where Pearl had grown up with Tealeaf as her maid. That story, told by Mam, had been hard to imagine. Now, faced with crumbling stone and planks of timber curled about with scrub, it was easier. Pearl had been real. She had faced dangers just as great as she and Ben were facing. With Hari, she had jumped off the cliff into the sea. So she, Hana, with Ben, could fight the Limping Man. But her confidence crumbled then, like the rotten wood under her fingers. What Pearl and Hari had done was in the past. For her and Ben the Limping Man lay ahead.

They crawled wide of the ruins, fearing snakes more than

the guards. The scrub thinned out, barely covering them. The ground grew rough with stones, which Hana recognised as broken paving. A road had run here in Ottmar's time.

They followed it, keeping their cover. In a moment they heard feet and the tapping of a stick.

Wait, Ben said. He crept away.

She followed him. They were too close now for her to be left behind.

The footsteps were a soldier's as he walked on a path through the scrub. He used his spear as a walking stick as he went along. Where the path curved he met another soldier and started back.

Same thing, Ben said. They don't turn until they see each other. This path must go down to the city.

They withdrew silently and worked their way towards the cliffs. In a moment the palace came in sight again. It was two storeys high, with a hump on its back. Palace: the word had meant, to Ben, a building rising high, with turrets and towers and statues carved in stone. This was a box. There were no windows. A narrow door, placed midway in the front wall, was flanked with torches burning in brackets. That was all. The moonlight showed walls that seemed to be red, with yellow flames eating them. The Limping Man came from the swamp but he liked fire.

Further off stood a barracks for the guards. Several small buildings rose where the lawn met the scrub.

Ben and Hana watched the guards trudge around the palace. They stopped at every corner, where each made two lazy salutes, one to the man ahead and one behind, before going on.

There was no way of getting to Vosper's box and no way of getting inside.

Dawn lit the sky over the mountains. They moved to the

back of the building, as far as the fountain. Ben crept further on to see the hidden side. Hana was sure he would find no way of getting inside there. She studied the building and felt more confident. With buildings, ruined or not, she knew what to do.

Ben, she said when he came back, that hump on top is a room and there are windows. He must live there.

So? How are we going to get up?

Climb.

How?

See the corners. Those blocks of stone stand out from the walls. I'll go up there.

It was a way he could not take, it needed two hands.

I'll tell you what I find. Go back to the front. Tell me when they change guards.

She thought he was going to argue, but at last he nodded. She saw he had a plan of his own.

Ben, don't.

He grinned at her but said nothing.

Please wait until I tell you.

Sure, he said. Send me a message.

If I can find out what Queenie knew . . .

When I kill him we won't need to know.

It was too late to argue. The sky was light and a shout of command came from the front of the building. Ben put his hand on her shoulder. He touched her cheek.

We'll both try, he said. And maybe . . .

He was saying goodbye. She returned his touch lightly, with her fingers beside his mouth. Then she laid her hand on the stump of his arm. She believed both of them would die.

'Goodbye, Ben,' she whispered.

'Listen for me. Then start climbing.'

He slipped away. The guards circled again. Then the one at

the front of the palace failed to appear. The man Hana could see completed his walk and went from sight, and Ben's voice sounded in her head: Now. Climb.

She ran. She went up the corner, hooking her fingers, leaning back on her arms, and as she mounted his voice came again: I'll meet you in the cave if we make it.

A wooden parapet circled the roof. She flopped over behind a row of ferns growing in tubs and lay catching her breath. Then she parted the fronds and looked at the wooden room squatting on the palace like a frog. The near-side window was barred and covered. What was inside? Frogs and toads? Had Vosper shifted them from the building by the cliff? He grew up in a swamp, she thought, so he brings the swamp with him. It made her shiver. Everything about the Limping Man made her shiver.

She circled the building below window height. There was a narrow door in the front. She turned the handle cautiously. It was locked, and barred on the inside, she guessed. She went to the back, away from the barracks, and risked looking in a window. It took a moment for her eyes to get used to the change of light. Then she saw a shallow trough running the length of the room. A row of cages stood opposite. If this was a toad-house the frogs and baby mice used as food would be kept there. Where were the toads? She looked at the trough again. Rocks rose from the water. It took her a moment to see that toads sat motionless on them, like rocks themselves. Their skins were mottled green with a red stripe down the back. Their sticky pads rested in front like human hands and their eyes, bulging with knowledge, never moved. She wondered if *they* ever moved, then saw others about the room, in corners and along the base of the cages. A small one – she gave a yelp – was watching her from the sill inside the mesh covering the window.

Hana backed away and crawled to her hiding place by the parapet. Toads, she thought. He brings the swamp with him. When would he feed them? She hoped no one would come to water the ferns.

Ben, she thought. She wanted to tell him what she had seen. She whispered his name. No answer came. She did not dare 'speak' loudly, not this close to the Limping Man.

Hunger began to trouble her. She drank water. The sun climbed but the drooping fernleaves kept her cool. The regular footsteps of the sentries became almost comforting.

She timed the hours. The palace stayed silent, until, at mid-morning, a rumbling came from deep in the building. She crept to a window. Her eye caught a movement in a narrow alcove in the front wall. Ropes were moving through pulleys fixed inside. Then she almost cried out: the Limping Man appeared. First his head, with his pink mouth smiling dreamily. His head-dress was gone. He wore a skull-cap on his wispy hair. His body, rising in the alcove, was swathed in a red cloak with a high collar. He rested on his stick as the platform rumbled up, and leaned on it stepping into the room.

Hana crouched, working out what to do. He would be busy at the cages, then with the toads. The back window was the safest place. She shifted there and when she looked again the Limping Man had leaned his stick against a cage door and was approaching the trough, with a struggling frog in each hand. His left side dipped at every step, he seemed on the point of falling, but his mouth kept its dreamy smile and his voice spoke liltingly: 'Breakfast, my lovely ones. Nice fat frogs for breakfast. See how Vosper loves you.' He held each frog by a back leg and dangled them over two large toads basking on the rocks. They raised themselves slightly. Each shot out a tongue the length of its body. For a moment the frogs bulged in their throats, then were gone.

The Limping Man laughed. 'Juicy ones,' he said.

Hana crouched below the window. She imagined herself rushing into the room and killing the Limping Man the way she had killed the bounty hunter. But the bars were strong, there was no way in. She looked again. He was feeding mice to the toads, holding them by their tails and offering them. The sticky tongues shot out and sprang back. The mice vanished. The Limping Man sang a little trill of delight.

If Ben was here he would find a way in. He would throw his knife and it would be over. Ben, she thought. The Limping Man gave a start. He lifted his hand and smacked the side of his head. Hana crouched. Her thought had touched him as though a fly had escaped from a cage and settled on his hair.

She must keep Ben out of her mind – everything out of her mind. She lay below the window, listening as he resumed the feeding of his toads. The cage doors creaked, his feet shuffled unevenly across the room. He took a long time. She heard him humming with enjoyment.

Say something, Vosper. Tell me your secret, she thought.

The sounds stopped. He had heard again. A toad splashed in the pool.

'Ma,' the Limping Man whispered, 'don't torment me.' He shuffled partway across the room. Hana rose on her knees and looked over the sill. The Limping Man was reaching out. He wanted his stick. Was that it? Was the secret of his strength in the carved stick?

'Ma,' he said again, 'you know what it is.'

He took another half dozen steps, grabbed the stick and leaned on it – and Hana waited, she had no idea what for. Something like a thunderclap? For his strength to roll over her like a wave? There was nothing. No change. He had needed his stick to save himself from falling, that was all.

He leaned on it and rested against the cages.

'You wanted to tell them, Ma, so I had to kill you.' He banged his stick on the floor. 'Betray me, would you, for a pigeon? You should have swallowed mud like Jug. You should have burned.' His pink face flushed with rage. Again he banged the stick. 'For an eel! A pigeon! No love, Ma. So you die. Go away now. Lie in the mud with Jug. Only my toads love me.' He made three steps towards the trough. 'So, my lovely ones, I bring fat mice and juicy frogs. And tomorrow I will burn some witches for you. That will be good. And when my armies march, the swamps and jungles will be yours.'

He laughed again. 'So go away, Ma. Vosper doesn't need you any more.'

Hana kept her thoughts quiet, even though he was so pleased with himself she doubted he had room to hear. He reached the tank. 'The world is ours, my lovelies. Lord Vosper of the Swamp. What banquets we will have. What burnings we will have.'

He stroked his finger down the red lightning flash on the back of the nearest toad. It watched him with its bulging eyes. How could he love these creatures? All they wanted was food, Hana thought. They would eat him too if he were small enough.

She stopped watching and lay below the window. Soon she heard the squeak of pulleys as the Limping Man sank into his palace. Light rain started to fall. She turned on her back and let it wash her. Wet on her face, cool on her face.

It was not enough to wash away the toads. And nothing would wash away the Limping Man.

TEN

The distance from the scrub to the palace door was too far. Ben wanted his throw to be hard and flat. A better place was in the scrub beside the path. But Vosper would be riding in his litter, with the curtains closed and guards on either side.

He crept back and forth several times. The door? The path? And when would Vosper come out of his palace? Perhaps not until the burnings tomorrow. Ben would snare some scrub quail if he had to wait that long, and go back to the cave for water. Hana would be down from the roof. He would leave her at the cave, tell her to get away – if she came down. He had a sick feeling she would not. It took him some time to shake it away.

He chose the door and settled in the scrub just off the lawn. Soft rain fell. He lay on his back and opened his mouth, catching drips from the leaves. Once he thought he heard her whisper his name, then decided he had been dreaming. There was no way she could come down until the sentries changed.

Hana, he thought. She was the strangest girl – the strangest person – he had known. It wasn't only that she was happiest alone – he understood that. It wasn't that she knew almost none of the things he knew. She had grown up in the burrows, how could she know? It was – he thought about it – that she wanted nothing. She was enough for herself. Like me, he thought; then knew he was wrong. He wanted her.

At first he had thought she was ugly, because of her eyes flecked with gold. Because of her thinness and wiriness. He liked plump girls. Now he liked Hana: her eyes and brown skin and hands as strong as his – and two of them where he had only one. He remembered her at the forest creek, without her clothes. One day, working in the gardens outside the village, he had seen Jed from the fishing boats walk by into the trees. Minnie slipped away from the bean rows after him. Ben followed. He saw what they did. From that day he had been ready himself. Was Hana ready? How could he find out a thing like that?

He lay with water dripping on his face. Stop, he thought, or you'll throw crooked when Vosper comes. He rolled on to his front and watched the palace door.

The rain stopped, the clouds melted and soon the stone path across the lawn steamed in the heat. The even tread of the sentry almost put Ben to sleep. It was a moment before he saw that the door had opened. A small man in black appeared like an insect from a hole. He raised his hand and a squad of soldiers assembled in front of the barracks. Four men in shining helmets and leather jerkins came out – the bearers. They opened double doors in another building, carried out the litter and set it on the grass, where the little man inspected it, fussing with the curtains. A squad of soldiers escorted them to the palace door.

Ben took out his knife and held it ready. He calculated the distance. It was too far. Unless he could get closer the knife would have to travel in an arc. But the soldiers had their crossbows armed. They would have a dozen bolts in him before he had gone five steps.

The crier came from the palace door and blew a trumpet blast. The Limping Man appeared – too far away, too far. Yet this was the closest Ben had seen him. Everything was the way Hana had described: the small face, the pink mouth, the watery eyes. The limp. The stick. The ceremonial robes that made him look like someone burning in a fire. For a moment he was clear in Ben's sight and if he threw from the edge of the scrub there was a chance. Only Hari and Duro, and Tarl the Dog King, who was dead, had knife skills equal to his. He edged closer in the scrub – but the moment had gone. The crier stepped across, and a second small man in black was also in the way. Ben sank into the wet bushes. He swore at himself – fisherman's curses. Hari and Duro would not have missed the chance.

He went deeper into the scrub, circling back to the path where it crossed the overgrown road. There was an easy throw there, he could hit Vosper where he chose – chest, throat or eye. But would the litter be open? A blind throw through the curtains was no use. He had to be certain of a kill.

Another trumpet blast came, followed by the tramp of feet on the path. Ben drew back. The scrub had wet his hand but the knife blade was dry and he was confident of his grip. Four soldiers appeared, marching in step. The crier followed. He was the biggest man Ben had ever seen. His naked sword shone like glass, his trumpet bounced on his hard belly as he walked. The little men in black pranced on either side of the litter.

The curtains were closed. They hung limp, almost brushing the path. And they were heavy. They would smother the knife before it passed through. And where was Vosper anyway? He might be lying down in there. He might be sleeping.

Ben waited until the soldiers at the back went from sight. The sentry, who had knelt beside the path as the litter passed, resumed his patrolling. Ben retreated deep into the scrub. He saw now what he must do. There was only one throw he could make. He planned it, played it over: the palace door, the moment Vosper stepped from the litter . . . The only question was, when would he come back?

The scrub dried out. Ben grew hungrier. He dug with his knife round the roots of a tree and found grubs. They were bitter and he spat them out. He wondered if Hana was hungry. He wondered if she was still alive. Would he have felt it if the Limping Man had killed her?

Midday. He crept back and looked at the palace. Vosper had grown up in the middle of a swamp but even so he should have built a better place than this. It was like a palace a child might draw – a box with a single door and flames painted on the sides. Maybe when he ruled the world he would build something better. But he's not going to rule the world, Ben thought.

Hana, he whispered. Silence. Heavy silence under the burning sun. He's got her, he thought. He'll burn her tomorrow with Blossom in the square. He stopped himself from running at the door to break it down.

A trumpet sounded distantly, jerking him back into good sense. The sentries circling the palace heard it too. They stood straighter and walked with a firmer step. He had not gone far, the Limping Man, just to the place called Ceebeedee. Ben checked his line of sight to the door. He cleaned a crumb of dirt off the blade of his knife.

The trumpet blew again, at the top of the path leading down to the city. In a moment the tread of marching men sounded on the paving stones. The first squad of four appeared, followed by the crier, who blew again, making

Ben's ears ring. The sentries stood to attention, one at each corner of the palace. The litter, red as fire, threaded out of the scrub. The bearers marched to the palace door and lowered it to the ground.

Ben checked his distance again. He would have to step out, get free of the scrub in a single step and make his throw. He visualised his knife the way Hari had taught him – saw its flight and the amount of height it would lose. He was ready.

The soldiers stood with their bows half raised. The crier walked to the door. The two men in black held the litter curtains, their white hands curled in the cloth. The crier banged the door with his sword handle.

'Open for the Limping Man,' he bellowed.

The door swung wide. The attendants at the litter pulled the curtains apart and the Limping Man put out his stick.

Not yet, Ben said. Wait until he's standing up. At this distance it had to be the middle of his chest.

The Limping Man struggled down. For a moment he was clear in Ben's sight – his white face, his damp eyes. His head-dress was like a rooster's comb, his robes, embroidered with flames, wrapped him round. One of the flames pointed at his heart.

Ben stepped out. No thought. As the knife left his hand he knew that Vosper was dead. It flashed in the sun, turning once, turning twice – and between the turns one of the attendants screamed like a baby and stepped with a click-beetle's speed in front of Vosper. The knife struck him high in the throat. He fell at Vosper's feet. The second attendant stepped over him with his arms flung wide, protecting his master.

The crier leapt down from the steps. Two of the soldiers shot. The bolts whizzed either side of Ben.

'Kill him,' shrieked the crier.

'No,' answered a piping voice. It stopped the crier, stopped the soldiers, it seemed to stop Ben breathing. All he could see was Vosper's face, peering out from behind the attendant.

'Leave him,' Vosper said.

Ben turned to run and had gone one step when something struck a blow deep in his head, something sharp and blunt at once, piercing him and crushing him. He felt his mind go dark and he fell and lay in shadows. He knew what was happening and also did not know – knew that feet rolled him over, knew guards dragged him by his heels across the grass until he lay beside the man he had killed. He tried to crawl away but could not move.

'Take this one away,' said the Limping Man, prodding the dead attendant with his stick. Two of the bearers dragged the body behind the litter. The Limping Man prodded again, shifting the man in front of him.

'Let me see this boy. Ha, one arm. I'm sorry for you, boy. Did it hurt?'

'Answer the Man,' the crier bellowed.

'Shh. Shh. He cannot,' said the Limping Man. 'I'll untie you a little, boy. But you must be good.'

Ben felt the numbing darkness lift from his mind. He tried to crawl towards Vosper. He meant to kill him.

'No, no,' the Limping Man said. 'Put your foot on him, Haggie. Try not to hurt him.'

The crier's foot came down on Ben's back, knocking the breath out of him.

'Send the men to their barracks,' the Limping Man said.

'Master . . .?'

'There are no more.'

'The paths? The roof?'

'None on the paths. None on the roof. You worry too much. Get rid of the men and then be quiet.'

The soldiers marched away, two of them dragging the attendant's body, with Ben's knife still in its throat.

'Now,' said the Limping Man, smiling at Ben with his pink mouth, 'tell me who you are.'

It took all Ben's strength to raise his head. He spat at the Limping Man. 'Vosper,' he croaked.

The Limping Man's face darkened, but in a moment he smiled again as though at a child.

'That used to be my name, boy. You learned it from my mother. And yours is . . .?'

Ben snarled, but suddenly, painfully, the darkness in his head increased, and he heard his voice whisper, 'Ben.'

'See, it pops out like a pip from a lemon. You can't hide anything from me. You visited my poor mother, Ben, you and the girl. To find out what? Who I am? You think I have a secret. There's no secret. People love me. They worship me. Did you know that? When I've wiped out your villages and killed the Dweller vermin in the north, the world is mine and I'll give it to those who follow me. Will you follow me, Ben?'

Ben managed to shake his head. He did not know the sound he made, meaning no.

'You're a stubborn boy,' said the Limping Man. 'I had to kill my mother because of you. She sold me for a fat pigeon. Poor Queenie. But never mind. I have Blossom and Hubert and I have you. What a pity the girl ran away. My men found her footprints in the sand. Betrayal, Ben. She turned her back on you the way Queenie did on me. Women, you see. They're good for nothing. But we'll find her when we march north, and punish her. What's her name, Ben?'

Ben could not help himself. He choked the name back but could not stop it.

'Hana,' he croaked.

'Hana. Well, Ben, Hana will burn. Be sure of it. But you, you will drown. Tomorrow, in the square. The numbers grow, Haggie. What a day it will be. Blow for the boy. Let him hear my sound.'

The crier raised his trumpet and blew a rough-edged blast until his breath ran out.

'Hear that, Ben? Your forests will ring with it. How can you not worship me? But you hate me still. I see it in your head, feeding like a worm. Let me get rid of it for you.'

No, Ben managed to think, and then the word made a wailing sound and faded away and in its place a picture grew: the Limping Man, his smiling face, his loving smile, his eyes blue like the sky, shining with the promise of happiness. Where was the word? Where was 'no'? It had vanished. Instead there was 'yes'. There was love instead. It splashed over him like warm water from a jug. He struggled to his knees in front of the glowing figure standing before him. Tears ran down his face as he cried his love.

'Man,' Ben cried. 'Master,' he cried.

'There, you see, it's easy. But that's enough,' the Limping Man said. 'Tomorrow you will drown. I prefer to have you hating me, it pleases the crowd. So – tie him, Haggie.'

The crier bellowed, 'Rope,' and a man ran out of the barracks with a coil on his arm.

'Tie him,' the crier said. 'Tight.'

The man fastened Ben's elbows behind his back. He tied his ankles. Still Ben tried to see his master. In spite of the pain he cried his love.

'Enough. Stop now, Ben. Let my men see the face of hatred.'

As suddenly as he had been mastered, Ben was free. This time the water that washed him flowed from a forest stream. The monstrous love fell away like dirt from his mind, leaving no hatred, only pity. He looked up at the Limping Man – the robes, the rooster's comb, the weak eyes and baby's mouth, and he thought, He's stupid, Vosper is. How can I stop him killing everyone?

He said, 'I'm sorry I didn't stick you. But someone will.'

'Not you, boy. No one, ever,' the Limping Man said. 'Bring him, Haggie. Put him with the others.'

He limped into his palace. The crier followed, dragging Ben by the rope that bound his feet. The bearers carried the litter away.

ELEVEN

Hana heard the trumpet blow and feet tramp evenly on the path. Keeping back from the parapet, she raised herself high enough to see the Limping Man's litter disappear into the scrub. Its colour dazzled her. The crier's sword flashed in the sun. The soldiers' jerkins gleamed like beetle wings. She knelt again. Her knees felt weak. How could anyone fight him? A boy with a knife and a girl with – nothing.

The roof was warm. She lay close to the ferns, ready to hide if she heard the hoist rumble. Ben was out there somewhere in the scrub. Or perhaps he had followed the Limping Man along the path, waiting for his chance. It would never come. Her eyes grew wet with pity – he was so full of courage that had no use. She knew that in the end Ben would attack, even if he had no chance. He would throw his life away.

'Ben,' she whispered.

She lay on the hot roof as the sun climbed up the sky. She would help him somehow. She would join him when he attacked and throw her own life away. But she must not be captured. Hana was terrified of being burned.

She thought of Mam – and Mam seemed to be watching

her. Mam crooning a lullaby. Mam in the shelter, in the firelight, with Hana sitting between her knees; her fingers soft one moment, hard the next, as she picked lice out of Hana's hair.

When Mam came to her this way, when Mam was watching, it was a caress. She felt it again – but differently, not tender, something sharp, cutting round her edges like a knife . . .

Hana sprang to her knees. She looked at the sky. Wiped her wet eyes. Looked again.

A small black dot was circling there.

'Hawk,' she whispered.

Hawk, she cried inside herself. Without thought she let herself go to him, as she had that first time on the hill. It was climbing a silver rope, it was changing her skin as she fitted behind his eyes. There was no greeting. That was not Hawk's way. He was here. He was with her. That was all. It had to be her way as well.

She saw what he saw: the palace roof, herself kneeling with her face raised to the sky. She saw the scrub, the broken hand, the abandoned building on the cliff, with waves foaming on the rocks below.

Ben? Where's Ben? she said.

Hawk swooped lower, searching the scrub.

Your wing? Hana said. But Hawk could only show what he saw. If he ever came to sit with her she would look at the wing and see how well it had healed. In the meantime he flew, that was enough.

Ben was lying on his side in the scrub. He seemed to be sleeping. The sun, at its highest, lit his legs and face. Hana wanted to go lower and see if there was a way of talking with him but Hawk turned away. She could not command him, he was not hers. He dived in a straight line down a zigzagging

148

path, into a city she had never seen – not the burrows but the place Company had built – and there she saw people on a cleared piece of land and saw them kneeling to the Limping Man. He stood by his litter, with guards on either side. The crier paraded in front, bellowing, and the kneeling men shouted their response, which Hana heard faintly with Hawk's ears: 'Man, Man, praise the Man.'

Higher, Hawk, she whispered. She did not want the Limping Man to notice him. He too wanted to leave this place. He flew over Ceebeedee and out over the plains, where men galloped horses and others marched in squadrons and bowmen shot bolts and arrows into targets. Hawk flew above the reach of arrows. He looped south over a city of tents with coloured roofs and pennants flying on poles. At noon the soldiers would make fires and cook their food. Their leaders would be resting now in their tents – the same eastern and southern chiefs Hana had seen in multi-coloured robes at the burning. She tried to spit at them but could not – she was Hawk up here, she was a guest. She felt his head turn and the Limping Man's army slid away like a tray on a table. The speed of Hawk's changed focus made her dizzy. He looked beyond the tents into a hollow between two hills, where something moved. It was a hare. She felt Hawk's hunger, and felt her own, but knew she had no place in the kill.

Hawk, I'm going, she whispered. Come back soon. At once she was on the palace roof, with slate under her shins and her body stiff from kneeling. She searched the sky westwards but Hawk was not there. He was on the ground, between the hills, tearing his prey. She could almost taste the warm flesh. Hawk, bring me some, she whispered. She crept behind the ferns, out of the sun, and drank some water – almost her last. She searched for insects in the stalks. Meat, she thought. Please bring me some.

Below her the sentries tramped round and round the building. How did they keep going? Why didn't they turn and walk the other way? Hana dozed and woke, dozed and woke, tormented by hunger. In spite of it she was happy – Hawk had come. She woke with a start from a dream in which he was searching, a dream in which he circled in the sky, crying forlornly. She crawled from her hiding place and lay in the sun. The stone roof burned but she stayed where he could see, wondering how many days he had spent searching as she and Ben travelled, as they slept in the cave and hid in Danatok's house.

I'm sorry, Hawk.

Then, distantly, she heard a trumpet cry. The Limping Man was coming. She needed to see. Hawk, she called urgently. Whatever Ben planned, he would do it now. If she could see where he was there might be a way of helping him.

Ben, she called. There was no answer. His whole mind now was getting ready for Vosper. His whole mind would be in his knife.

Hana waited, watching for Hawk, feeling for Ben. Another trumpet blast: the Limping Man was close. She felt like an insect in a jar, knowing nothing of the world outside.

Feet tramped on the path through the scrub. They came to the palace door. She heard the litter creak as the bearers put it down.

Ben, don't, she whispered – then tried to withdraw the words. Whatever he would do, there was no place in his mind for her. Hawk, she said, I need to see.

Three heavy bangs shook the palace. The crier's voice bellowed, 'Open for the Man.' No sound of a door, but the swish of curtains opening. The Limping Man was stepping from his litter.

Hana waited. She pleaded for Hawk to come . . .

A grunt. Was that Ben? A scream like a seabird's cry. The whirr of crossbow bolts and a shout from the crier: 'Kill him.' Then a small voice, a whistling, childish voice, saying, 'No.'

How fast her brain was. She felt the bolts strike Ben, and strike her; but 'no' meant they had missed and he was alive. She had to see, and she raised her eyes again to the sky. Hawk was there. He found her as she found him. At once she climbed the silver rope and shared his eyes.

Everything was clear. She saw Ben lying face down, trying to crawl. She saw a small man dressed in black lying on the grass with a knife in his throat. She saw the buttons on his jacket and blood leaking into the cloth. He was meant to be the Limping Man. But the Limping Man leaned on his stick. He leaned and searched. She felt his mind rolling like a fog down the path and across the scrub; it climbed the palace walls and spread across the roof, over the toad-house and over her kneeling form as she stared at the sky. It ran over her and found nothing to touch. She had climbed the rope. Her mind was in the sky with Hawk.

Soldiers dragged Ben by the heels and laid him in front of the Limping Man. Hawk gave a twist of his tail, sliding across the scrub and sliding back.

Go down lower, Hana whispered. She wanted to hear what Vosper said. Was Ben speaking too? The crier stamped on him.

Lower, Hawk, please.

Hawk took no notice. There were times when he heard and times when he did not. He had fought for her in the forest but he would not go lower for Ben. So Hana left him; slid her mind down the sky into her own body. For a moment she was dizzy and stayed on hands and knees. Then she crawled to the parapet and hid in the ferns. She raised her head as Vosper, in his unbroken voice, said, 'Hana will burn.'

How did he know her name? Had he plucked it from Ben's mind? What else did he know?

The crier blew a long blast, making her ears ring. She heard only faintly what happened next – someone speaking. Then she heard Ben cry, 'Man. Master,' and she covered her ears to keep out the dreadful sound. The Limping Man had taken Ben's mind. It was worse than killing him. It was like making Ben one of his toads.

No, Ben, she whispered. Come back.

She listened again, and still he cried, 'Master,' in a voice full of devotion. She stopped her ears. She heard no more, except, distantly, the thud of a closing door.

It was a long time before she risked looking over the parapet. A sentry walked by, slow and lazy. That was all. She looked at the sky.

Hawk was gone.

TWELVE

Rain clouds boiled up from the west. Heavy drops splashed on the roof. Hana drank the last of her water and filled the bottle from the gutter inside the parapet. Her hunger did not matter, she was used to it. What mattered was bringing Ben back and the only way to do it was to kill the Limping Man. If he came to feed his toads again she would get in through a window. She tried to work one of the bars loose with her knife. The point snapped off. She knelt with the rain beating on her head. Not even a knife. Perhaps tomorrow she could hide in a building in the burrows and tip a heavy stone on to the litter . . . But she did not know which streets he would pass through, and even if she did, no stone would kill the Limping Man.

Hawk, help me, she pleaded.

The rain stopped and the clouds rolled away. He was nowhere in the sky.

Hot sun. She lay on the roof, ignoring the shade of the ferns. Her clothes steamed and her hair dried on the slates. Ben was somewhere in the palace below, perhaps crying his devotion still. If the Limping Man questioned him he would say she was on the roof. She had the horrible thought that Vosper might send Ben to kill her. The only way then would be to jump from the parapet and, if her legs did not break, run for the scrub. Where to after that? She imagined Ben coming after her – a Ben she did not know, horribly changed. She would try to wrestle him off the cliff. They would fall like Pearl and Hari. Pearl and Hari had lived. They would die.

If Hawk would only lift me up and fly away . . .

Hana slept, and when she woke he was waiting beside her. He lifted his claw off a fat pigeon lying by her head.

'Ah, Hawk . . .'

She plucked its feathers and cut off a leg, which she offered him. He refused. She peeled the skin and ate the flesh, then sliced tender meat from the breast and ate that too. Hawk accepted the carcase after that. He opened it with his beak and found the heart and liver. Hana poured water into her hand and held it out. He drank, scooping with his lower beak, then flew away. Hana waited for the sun to go down. It touched the sea, turning red and shooting an arrow of light along the horizon.

Shouted orders came from the front of the palace. She crept to the back; found Hawk in the sky; joined him and watched until the sentries were lined up outside the palace door. She hurtled down the silver rope and shook herself into her own body. Monkey-quick, she climbed down the corner of the building and ran for the scrub, where she burrowed in and waited until the sentries resumed their march. Then she crept to the hand. The last of the sun turned it pink, and there was Hawk, perched on the broken finger.

Where do you sleep, Hawk? Where do you go?

They were questions for herself.

Will you find me in the morning? I don't know where I'll be.

His feathers shone in the last shooting rays – red, green, gold – then he spread his wings (she saw no wound) as if trying them, sprang into the air and flapped away. Hana heard a sentry approaching on the path. She retreated into the scrub, which was full of black pools now the light was gone. She felt her way through, although it would be safer to wait until the moon came up. But she did not want to stay near the palace. All day she had lain on the roof, close to Vosper and his toads. She wanted to get away from the contagion that had claimed Ben.

She passed the burned mansion, passed the other fallen houses, and as she went felt the Limping Man's influence decrease. She felt sick at leaving Ben there.

'I'll try, Ben, I'll try,' she whispered; and could not make sense of her words.

Hana reached Bawdhouse Burrow as the sun rose. There was no change – the same rubble heaps, the same broken stairways, the same scummy pools in the parks, with weeds spreading on them, half-closing them like eyes. Women were usually out at dawn, drawing water from the single well. Today they stayed in their shelters, keeping their children close, keeping quiet. If the burning quota was not full the constables would take any woman they saw. She found the crawl to the shelter she had shared with Mam and rested there a few steps from the street. Sleep was hard. Fear crept into her mind with every breath. But Mam was with her too. Mam placed a cool hand on her brow. Hana, she whispered, the weed.

Hana understood. If she had frogweed she would be safe. If constables found her she could die like Mam. She crawled until she reached the stone blocking the shelter. There were no voices inside, no life. A man would be gone already to

People's Square but a woman would be moving about and children playing. She put her feet on the rock, straightened her legs and rolled it away. Silence again. She crept into the room where she had spent most of her life. No one lived there now. The family that had moved in was gone. The bunk lay smashed. The fire corner was cold, the ashes grey. Nothing remained except . . . Hana advanced. The pot stood on the shelf. Leaves of frogweed drooped down its sides. They crumbled when she touched them. The weed was dead.

Hana sat on the cold floor and wept. Soon Mam spoke to her again.

Hana, I told you to go far away.

'Yes, Mam,' she said.

But you came back.

'Yes,' she snuffled.

So now you must be brave.

'How?' she said.

Was it Mam who answered or was it herself?

You've still got Hawk.

She wiped her arm across her face. She stood up and left the shelter, not using the crawl but stepping into the street. The sky was half white with clouds and half blue. No Hawk. He would be hunting. She wondered if he would bring her another pigeon. But it seemed wrong to think of eating on the day Ben would die – Ben and Blossom and Hubert and all the others. And apart from bringing food, how could Hawk help her? Perhaps only by finding a place where she could run at the Limping Man with her broken knife.

If that's the only way, that's what I'll do, Hana thought.

She made her way towards People's Square, using the route Mam had taught her. Crouching in doorways, she watched men go by. They crowded and jostled each other, but all were jovial. Some were soldiers enjoying a day's leave before they marched. She felt them simmering with the pleasures waiting for them in the square, and the chance of killing and plunder after that. The word she heard most frequently was 'Man'.

At the next turning, she found Mam's way blocked so she slipped into ruined streets and climbed through broken buildings. Hawk might have shown her an easier way but he did not come. What had Mam meant – and was it Mam who spoke or was it her own voice? – when she told her she still had Hawk? Hawk brought her food, he was her spy, and he had attacked the bounty hunter, but she could not imagine how he might help her fight the Limping Man. Several times she climbed high in buildings and stood on roofs. She wanted Hawk for company but he was nowhere in the sky.

I've got to be without him, Hana thought. She would find a window, jump on the litter when it passed. Kill the Limping Man with her broken knife. She retreated into the back rooms of a building and sharpened the blade on a stone. Where would the best place be? Both Hari's tale and Xantee's spoke of a hole in the floor over the western gate into People's Square. She had seen Vosper's litter enter that way on the day Mam died.

Hana got her bearings and worked towards it, through rooms with fallen ceilings and leaning walls. She entered a room so huge that its far end was lost in darkness. The floor was grey with dust and grit yet seemed to have puddles here and there, not of moisture but of colour and light. She advanced cautiously, knife ready, then stopped at the first patch of light and drew in her breath. Not puddles, not just light, they were pictures made of coloured stones fitted side by side. This must be the ballroom in the story Mam had told her, Hari's story. The whole floor, under the dust and rubble, was one huge picture of – everything. Someone had swept parts of it clear. Here was a farmyard with a man feeding hay to cattle; here a kitchen with a cook turning a pig on a spit; a golden fish swimming in a stream; a child – a laughing child – sitting in a small cart with wheels; a pigeon diving, a great golden hawk in pursuit . . . it went on and on: a man with a plough, a woman tying up her hair, lovers embracing. Who had uncovered it all, and what lay left to be uncovered? Hana felt whoever it was would not threaten her. She sat down next to the woman tying her hair. It could be Mam. She dreamed a while – Mam and Hawk, a forest stream, a little house to live in, Ben bringing fish from the stream . . .

'Girl,' a voice whispered behind her. She gave a half-scream, leapt to her feet, freed her knife. A figure approached from the dark end of the room.

'Girl,' he said, 'put away your knife. You know who I am. Where is my son?'

'Lo,' she gasped. 'Ah, Lo.' She ran to him and hugged him and after a startled moment he hugged her back.

'Girl, you should be far away. There's nothing you can do here.'

'Kill him. I can kill the Limping Man.'

'No. Leave it to others. Leave it to Blossom and Hubert.'

'He's got them. He captured them. He'll burn her today and drown him. Lo, he's got Ben. He makes Ben call him Master. I heard. I've got to save Ben.'

She thought for a moment he would crumple to the floor. He covered his face – old brown hands, jungle hands, hiding his grief. He looked half the size she remembered – starved and wrinkled and grey-haired. But after a moment he dropped his hands. His eyes were fierce and he said, 'Then I must do it.'

'Do what, Lo?'

'Fight the Limping Man.'

'You can't. Blossom and Hubert tried. We saw them. He just' – she kicked a stone aside – 'did that to them. And Ben tried to kill him and now he says Master.'

'There are ways. I'll try my way.'

'What is it?'

'Something I've been thinking of. When I left you I tried to speak with the people. I wanted to ask for their wisdom and their strength. But they were too far. I heard only a whisper. So I came here. This is the room Hari told us about when we were children. I came to see the coloured stones and speak with the people on the floor. See, Hana, this woman combing her hair, and this one tying wheat sheaves, and this one suckling her baby. See this man ploughing and this man sowing, and this girl milking her cow. I talked with them instead of the people. Come with me.'

He led Hana across the room to where a band of light lay across the floor.

'Mostly I talked with her.'

It was a simple picture: a woman in a blue dress crossing a wooden bridge over a stream. Her black hair hung about her shoulders. She held out her cupped hands as though offering something. They were empty, and yet they held everything pictured on the floor. Hana felt her throat thicken and her eyes grow wet.

'Does she tell you what to do?'

'She tells me this is how things were and might be again. What I will do . . .' He sighed.

'You don't know.'

'I've sat here three days, Hana. All of this is in me. I don't know whether it's enough.'

'Against . . .?'

'Him.'

'Against the swamp,' she said.

159

She offered Lo water. He drank a little. 'Now Hana, you must get away.'

'Are you going to fight him?'

'I'm going to try.'

'Blossom and Hubert –'

'I'm different from them. I've lived with the people. And there is . . .' He swept his hand at the shining pictures on the floor. 'Now leave me. I need to be alone. Promise me you'll find a place far away.'

'With Hawk?'

'Ah, Hawk is back. Yes, with him. And we'll find you, Ben and I.'

She did not believe it. She made no promise, but touched his face as she had touched Ben's and went away. For a short while she retraced her steps. Then she circled away from the ballroom, sometimes climbing, sometimes diving into basement rooms. Twice she crept by gaps where windows opened on People's Square. It was thronged with people. She saw the Limping Man's throne, with men in robes of every colour seated around it. At a third window she glimpsed – and turned away – two rows of stakes with wood piled at the foot. More stakes than last time. Men, burrows men, crowded close. They were so many that some stood up to their knees in the green pond.

Hana heard a rumble of expectation. It meant the Limping Man was close. She crawled and climbed and reached the hole above the western gate. A guard lounged there, facing the hole, resting his spear butt on the ground. He would stand straight when the Limping Man passed. It would be her signal. She edged towards him.

Tramping feet. A squadron. They marched into the square and the sound was lost in a wave of cheering. The generals came next, and rising above the shouts that greeted them, a trumpet blast. The guard beside the hole lifted his spear in a salute. Hana saw the red of the litter reflected in its point.

'Praise the Man,' he cried.

She drew her knife, drew her breath, and ran at him; struck him with her stiffened arm, propelled him into the hole and rode on his back down to the litter. His spear broke under him as he struck its roof. His weight tore the poles from the bearers' grip. The litter crashed to the ground. The guard's shoulder in Hana's ribs knocked her breath away, but she kept hold of her knife and started ripping the crimson cloth, knowing only that the Limping Man was inside and she must kill him. Knowing too, as the knife found no bite, that she had failed. The litter had a wooden roof beneath the cloth. She reached over the edge, screaming and slashing, trying to find a way through the side curtains.

Hands gripped her and dragged her down.

She heard the crier bellow, 'Kill the bitch.'

'Yes,' she heard her own voice say, pleading not to be burned. But there was another voice, soft and reasonable and sweet: 'No, don't hurt her. Treat her gently.'

Hana looked into the face of the Limping Man.

'Stand her up. Let me see.'

The bearers pulled the unconscious guard from the roof of the litter and dragged him aside. The Limping Man was level with Hana, holding red curtains under his chin, framing his face.

'Vosper,' Hana whispered. She tried to spit at him but her mouth was dry.

'Yes, indeed,' smiled the Limping Man. 'And you are Hana, who ran away but did not run. You should not have turned back, my dear.'

'Someone will kill you,' she managed to say.

'Oh no, never,' he said. 'But we have no time for talking.

I won't make you love me, like Ben. Today my people want hatred, that is best. Haggie.'

'Master?' the crier said.

'Tell them to raise another stake.' He took an edge of his curtain and wiped his watery eyes. 'And put it in the centre, Haggie. She's a brave girl and deserves a special place. Blow a loud blast for her. Blow two.'

He smiled at Hana and raised his finger. The attendant closed the curtain and the bearers made ready to move.

Two men held Hana. They pulled her upright when she stumbled. Haggie blew the trumpet, and blew a second time. Colour, shouting, grinning mouths, the stink of men packed together like rushes in a swamp. She was in People's Square. The sky opened up, blue like the woman's dress in the ballroom. Hana raised her head, trying to free herself from the thick noise and hungry faces.

A tiny black dot stood motionless above her.

Hawk was there.

THIRTEEN

They chained her to a post set in front of the others and packed dry wood round her feet. The Limping Man smiled down from his throne. He seemed no more than an arm's length away. The crier shouted and a pathway opened in the crowd. Four men with their arms tied were whipped and driven through and thrown in a heap at the edge of the pool. Then came Danatok, with torn clothes and ragged hair and hanging head. Hana cried his name. He did not look up. Nor did Hubert, walking behind with a heavy step. He did not seem to know where he was.

Ben came last. He struggled, he kicked, he tried to bite. Hana felt a surge of love and pride. He was free from the Limping Man.

They threw him with the others and because he still fought bound him with extra cords. He rolled at the guards and lashed out with his tied feet at their legs. Then he saw Hana and gave a cry of rage and loss.

'Ben,' she called. There was nothing to say but his name.

Guards brought in the women, twenty of them, old and young, weeping and pleading. Several seemed drugged. A few were stoical. And Blossom was like Hubert, she walked as though she did not understand her feet, so deep was the Limping Man's hold on her.

Hana could not bear to watch. She found Hawk in the sky and fled to him.

Fly away, Hawk. Fly, she said.

He circled lower. She saw People's Square like a basin. The crowd, the green pool, the stands, the throne. The litter, at the foot of the steps, flickered in the breeze like a fire. Ben struggled with the cords binding him.

Guards chained the women to their posts. A trumpet blast wound into the sky. It seemed to jar Hawk – perhaps hurt the wing that bent a little more crookedly than the other. He side-slipped across the square in a way that made her dizzy and when she looked again the crier was at the head of the stairs shouting at the crowd. The breeze crossing the square blew his words away. 'Witch,' she heard, and 'tried to kill our master' and 'cannot die' and 'forever'. There was much more. The crowd's roar rose in a blast that tossed Hawk back across the square.

The Limping Man raised his hand and the crier fell silent. He went to Vosper's side and sank to his knees to listen. Then he beckoned the bearers kneeling to one side. They lifted the throne and carried it to the steps, adjusted their hold, the front pair raising the poles as they went down. The Limping Man seemed to float as he descended . . . and then Hawk's eye caught something else, making Hana dizzy again. He watched the pool. A ripple on its surface flowed from the farthest edge towards the marble head with the crying mouth. Rat, Hana thought.

Hawk? she asked.

Why did he watch?

No one in the square saw. Every eye was locked on the

164

Limping Man as his bearers carried the throne down the steps, adjusted their hold and crossed the cobbles to where Hana slumped against the chains holding her. Hawk flicked a look and turned back to the pond. For a moment Hana thought he was going to dive at the rat as it reached the statue.

No, Hawk.

He banked lower. Something broke the surface: a grey head. It paused at the back of the statue – and Lo raised his face, took a breath and sank again.

Ha, Hana cried. She wished she had a voice. Lo had found the hole where Hari had escaped from the Company Whips. He was swimming to confront the Limping Man.

I'm going, Hawk. Stay here. Please don't go.

She plunged down the sky into her body. The bearers reached the stake where she was chained and the Limping Man grounded his stick, bringing a sudden hush over the square. Shouts of praise burst out again as he struggled to his feet. A wind was whipping over his head and rushing down, making his robes dance and his head-dress swell. Painfully, he walked the last few steps to Hana's stake. He flicked his hand at the crier, walking behind. The man stepped back and swelled his throat.

'Silence,' he cried and the crowd grew as still as water in a pond.

'Further back, Haggie. I want to talk with her,' said the Limping Man. He reached out and touched Hana's cheek. 'What a pity,' he said.

'Spit, Hana. Bite him,' Ben screamed. One of the guards kicked him in the ribs.

'I would save you if I could,' said the Limping Man.

'How?' Hana whispered.

'Easily enough. Not from death. Only pain.'

'How?'

He smiled at her. He had the face of a kind old man, yet he was not much older than Lo. Where was Lo?

'You should not have gone to Queenie, my dear. She didn't know my secret. She only guessed.'

Hana wet her mouth. 'How will you stop the pain?'

'The witches' way. You know the frogweed? My men will fetch some. You can chew before they light the fires. No pain, Hana. Your body will burn but you'll be dead. All you have to do . . .'

Where was Lo?

The Limping Man gave his sweet smile. '. . . is worship me.'

She did not understand. Again the wind whipped into the square, swirling his robes, rocking his head-dress. Without the band holding it under his chin it would fly away. She looked into the sky. Hawk was still there. Would he dive to save her the way he had with the bounty hunter? She lost some of the Limping Man's words.

'. . . make you fall on your knees if I wish. But I want you to do it without compulsion. I want you to do it because I'm worthy of your love.'

'And you'll give me the weed?' she whispered.

'Yes, my dear, for you to chew. Then, no pain.'

She wanted to say yes. She wanted him to send men for the frogweed – but she remembered Mam and she could not. Again she wet her lips.

'You are mud from the swamp,' she said.

His soft white face turned the colour of his robes. His eyes leaked water and his pink mouth snarled, showing brown backward-sloping teeth. He raised his stick to strike her but his leg would not hold. The crier jumped to support him. A dreadful silence fell on the square.

The Limping Man pushed his face at Hana. His spittle fell on her lips. 'Then burn and like it,' he said. He shook Haggie off. 'Save her till last. Let her hear the others.' He limped to his throne. The wind puffed his robes, making him fat. Hana saw his red shoes stepping on the cobbles.

Haggie blew a trumpet blast. 'Praise him,' he cried.

The shout began – and changed to a huge breath of disbelief. It was like a sob. Single shouts came from the crowd. Hana twisted her head to see where the fingers were pointing.

Lo rose from the edge of the pond. Weed draped his shoulders. Water leaked from his hair. A green man, naked, empty handed, he stepped from the mud on to the cobbles.

'Vosper,' he said.

The Limping Man turned. 'Who . . .?' he began; then nothing more as Lo raised his hand.

'See, Vosper, I limp like you. But I don't want to be king and conquer worlds.'

The words were not important. The struggle had already begun. Hana saw waves of force coming from both men and roiling where they met, like muddy water and clean water. The wind, leaping into the square, blew a deadly silence across the crowd. Lo was drawing his strength from the people, as much as they were able to give, from the forests, from the beaches, from the men and women working and dancing on the stone floor, from the sucking baby, from the cupped hands. Perhaps he also heard the voice that Hari and Pearl and Xantee had heard.

What did Vosper hear? His red angry face turned white. He leaned on his stick and did not totter, but drew strength from his worshippers. Hana felt him sucking it out of them. They drooped. They scarcely breathed. He drew it from the swamps. And somewhere else, somewhere else. Vosper heard the other voice. He seemed to swell as the wind ballooned his robes.

Hana felt the roiling increase. She saw Lo step back, find his balance on the wet cobbles, step forward again, holding his hands cupped, asking for strength. His toes gripped and his scarred leg strained. Grey-faced, lips drawn back, he fought to hold the tide rolling at him.

The dark water began to discolour the blue.

Ben, Hana pleaded. He was on his knees, pushing the little strength he had into his father. Hana added her own. Blossom too, Hubert too, groggy still, but partly released, tried to help.

It was not enough. Slowly, slowly, the Limping Man forced Lo to his knees. The cupped hands parted, spilled their life, as Lo leaned to support himself. They slid on the cobbles and he gave a cry of despair. His face banged on the stones and he lay still, except for the twitching of his crippled leg.

'See,' the Limping Man whispered.

'See!' bellowed the crier. 'Worship him. Worship the Man.'

The strength sucked out of them flowed back into the crowd. They shrieked like fangcats. They flung their arms in the air. Some fainted in ecstasy and sank in the sea of faces all around. The Limping Man let it go on. At last he raised his stick and the crier lifted his trumpet and blew. Silence. Terrible silence. Hana wept.

The Limping Man whispered to the crier, who stepped forward, pointed his sword and bellowed at the crowd: 'This man is the consort of witches. Their leader. He will drown in the water he came from. He will go first. This girl' – he swung to Hana – 'is the chief witch. For all her youth. The last of them. She will burn when the others have burned. You will hear the evil spirit scream as it flees from her. And then, my people, the world is yours to use as you wish, while you continue to worship me.'

The roar of love mounted like a cumulus cloud. The Limping Man regained his sweetness. He smiled at Hana like a little old woman. It filled her with horror – his transformation. She fled into the sky, fled to Hawk and trembled there, behind his eyes, seeing nothing for a moment. Then she looked at herself, chained to the stake; at Ben, tied at the elbows and feet, crawling like a crushed insect at Lo, and Lo, struggling to kneel and falling back. Vosper too – she saw him limping towards his throne at the foot of the steps.

A gust of wind jolted Hawk sideways. Down in the square it whipped across the crowd, over the women tied to their stakes, ballooned the Limping Man's robes, puffed out his head-dress – and Hawk's focus changed. Where was he looking? Why there? Why the head-dress? It seemed to throb and stir and rearrange itself as if something alive . . . A picture of a sun-warmed rock came into Hana's mind, floating as though under water, with small ants at the foot, tearing flesh from a dropped fish bone; then warriors bursting out to fight invaders, and killing them, except for one with a mite riding in the joint between its body and head. The mite, the rider?

Hana clamped her mind on Vosper's secret.

Hawk, she cried, but had no need. He was diving. She raced away from him, into her body, and saw Hawk falling out of the sky. He came like a stone towards the pond. He seemed to be aiming at the statue.

Hawk, she whispered. Again there was no need. His wings snapped out, half their reach, he sped across the pond, over the staked women, over Hana, to where the Limping Man had begun to turn. Slow, slow, and Hawk was fast. His claws were hooked. They caught the scarlet head-dress, pulled it from Vosper's head, with its fastening band and its waterfall of cloth. Hawk jerked in his flight, was frozen in the air for a moment, but struck downwards with his wings, once, twice, three times, and climbed above the Limping Man. The cloth trailed from his claws as Vosper screamed. Hawk rose across the cobbles and the crowd, with the scarlet streamer trailing behind. He dropped it and it opened like a flower as he turned.

There was more. There was the green toad with the blood-red stripe on its back, clinging to the Limping Man's shoulders.

The crowd breathed out, a prolonged whisper. The crier's trumpet clanged on the cobbles. The toad remained placid, his mouth fastened on the back of Vosper's neck. And Vosper dropped his stick, put his hands up to the creature and gave another cry when he felt its skin.

Hawk turned. He dived again, claws extended. They hooked into the toad and he flapped and flapped again, but the creature's sticky pads kept their hold on Vosper's neck. Vosper locked his hands on its back legs. Hawk beat. He beat his wings. Hawk was stronger. The pads came free. The back legs slid from Vosper's grasp. But still Hawk could not rise with the toad. Its tongue was buried deep in Vosper's neck, under the skull bone. As Hawk whacked the air with his wings it began to stretch, but the toad held on. The crier drew his sword.

Hana put her strength into Hawk. She did not know how, but she touched him as though with her hands. It was enough. With a wet sound the tongue came free and sprang back into the toad's mouth. Hawk rose with the creature in his claws. It beat the air with its pads, its back legs paddled. Hawk went higher. He rose over Hana's stake until he reached the height of the buildings round the square. The toad made a squeaking noise as Hawk let it go. It tried to inflate itself, lighten itself.

But it fell like a bladder full of liquid and burst on the stones at Hana's feet.

She turned her eyes away. The Limping Man – he was the one. What was the Limping Man doing? But he was gone. Vosper stood in his place, a little man in scarlet clothes, turning aimlessly. His feet slid, he sank to the ground, mumbling to himself and wiping his eyes.

Too many things happened then for Hana to remember with clarity. Some, perhaps, she had not seen, and Ben had told her, or Lo or Blossom; but she felt the memories were her own. Lo took back his strength as Vosper lost his. He rose to his feet, robbed a stunned soldier of his sword and cut Ben free. Ben darted past the crier, scattered the wood at Hana's feet with a kick, unhooked the chain that held her hands behind the post, hugged her against his chest for a moment, then ran to free Blossom and all three set about unhooking the other women. Lo cut the cords tying Hubert and Danatok.

Meanwhile the men on the stands, the men on the cobbles and around the pool, began to stir, the slow stir of an animal waking from hibernation. They began to grunt and clear their mouths and spit, to clamp and unclamp their hands and flex their knees. They shook their heads, shaking the Limping Man out. Some began to cry. Their cheeks grew wet with tears. Others turned round and round as though their heads were empty and their balance gone. They fell. They stood up. Some walked to the gates of the square and walked away. Others cried with shame at their captivity. And many looked for someone to kill. They clambered from the stands, they churned through the edges of the pool. On the cobbles, by his throne, they found the Limping Man.

Hana, Ben, Lo, Blossom, Hubert, Danatok: they stood in a knot. They were tiny in the crowd. There were men, hundreds of men, pulling each other, knocking each other aside, fighting for a place about the litter and the throne. Timber cracked. The scarlet roofs sank into a sea of shouting faces and clenched hands.

'Stop,' Lo cried. His voice was swallowed. He turned and started up the steps to the place where Vosper had sat. Ben followed with Hana, then Danatok and Blossom. Hubert paused long enough to snatch the crier's trumpet from the cobbles. They reached the platform. Some of the tribal leaders had fled to the gates, others had joined the maelstrom around Vosper. The stands were bare.

'Stop,' Lo cried again; but nothing could stop or alter the last act of the Limping Man's reign. Hands lifted him, held him high. Perhaps he was dead already. His robes rucked about his thighs, his shins, thin as sticks, gleamed in the sun.

'Don't let them,' Hana said. Lo shook his head.

They carried Vosper to the pool and held him under the water with hands and feet. All Hana saw of him was an edge of scarlet robe lost a moment later as men tramped it down. Then nothing but churned water and screaming faces.

Vosper was dead. The crowd drowned Haggie the crier and the attendant. Then they looked for other victims and found the bearers huddled by the wreckage of the litter.

Hubert had been trying to blow mud out of the trumpet. Hana found a stick and hooked it out. Hubert blew.

The men knew the sound. It froze them and before they could react and storm the stands, Ben seized the trumpet and hurled it into the air. It landed on the cobbles by the toad, where a man grabbed it and smashed it against one of the stakes.

'No more trumpets,' Ben cried. 'Now listen to my father.'

Lo did not raise his hands or shout, but spoke in his normal voice, which travelled easily across the crowd.

'Your king is dead. Now it's time for you to leave this place. Leave these men, the bearers, they were his slaves as much as you. You men from the south, take your armies home. Throw away your weapons, fight no more. And you city men, leave the burrows and Ceebeedee. These places are dead. Go into the plains. Make farms. Make villages. Fish the seas. Forget this city and the man who made you slaves – the man who made you hate your wives. Free them too, free the women. Without them you are half, you are less than the toads in the swamp. Go. Go now. And remember, no more kings.'

'You be our king,' someone cried.

'No!' Lo's voice was raised at last. It was like Haggie's trumpet. 'You are free. No more kings. No limping men.'

They trickled away – the leaders from the south, the city men, the burrows men. Slowly they went, all of them silent, some still crying, some half stunned. They trod over the green and red puddle made by the toad. People's Square was empty, except for Hana and her friends sitting at the top of the stairs.

Vosper, the Limping Man, floated face down in the green pool, with Haggie the crier on one side and the attendant on the other. Beyond them the sunken statue shouted at the sky.

Hana looked for Hawk. He was sitting on the chimney she had climbed on the day Mam died.

Mam, she said.

Hawk, she said.

He preened his shining feathers in the sun.

FOURTEEN

They climbed out of the city over the hill. Vosper's palace was ransacked. The tanks in the toad-house were smashed and the toads all dead. Burrows mice ran about the floor.

Beyond the swamp they met bands of men travelling aimlessly. Some were savage, some confused, and none could understand the emptiness they felt. Lo repeated his message. He and Blossom and Hubert kept a close watch. Once they found a hacked body and once a man hanging in a tree.

'Nothing's going to change, is it?' Hana said.

'Vosper's gone,' Blossom said.

'They'll make a new king. They don't want to be free.'

'Some do. Some don't.'

'There won't be an invasion, so we're safe,' Ben said.

He was unhappy with himself. Vosper had enslaved him so easily. Sometimes Hana caught him looking at his new knife as though it were the old and had let him down.

'He was stronger than Blossom and Hubert,' she said. 'He was stronger than Lo.'

'He was only a toad,' Ben said.

'No,' Blossom said, overhearing. 'He used the toad. It

wasn't feeding on him, he was feeding on it. Taking all that hunger and greed. And I think he heard his voice through it, swollen like a toad. Vosper won't come back.' She cupped her hands like the hands of the woman Hana and Lo had seen on the ballroom floor. Hana wondered if she believed a picture would be enough.

Northwards, then west towards the Inland Sea. Danatok left them, heading for Stone Creek.

'Can I fly with Hawk and see you?' Hana said.

'If you can find me.' He pressed her hands in his three-fingered ones, smiled with his cat eyes, and went away.

There were no more bands of men. The forests were safe. Hana and Ben sat on a rock high on a hill. The sun was low. Ben was looking at his knife again.

'Put it away,' she said.

Hawk dropped down and hovered over them.

'He won't come as long as you're unhappy.'

Ben put the knife in its sheath. Hawk sat by Hana on the rock. The next afternoon he landed between them and Hana was not jealous when he let Ben touch the feathers on his damaged wing. Ben grew happier after that.

The Dwellers at the Inland Sea had the boat ready to sail. With five of them there was little room but the sea stayed calm and a breeze blew steadily behind them. Hawk perched on the bow by Hana at night.

Pearl and Hari were waiting on the shore. Xantee and Duro were there with their children. Lo was easier now. He could say names. He would stay, and go when he needed to, and come back when they called. Blossom and Hubert, quiet and still, wondering at their defeat by Vosper, stayed on too. They were not unhappy, they were stronger and more rested than before.

Pearl and Hari had their family round them for the first time since the gool. Ben was part of it. And Hana, new and uneasy at first – a family had been her and Mam – fitted in gradually. She spent a lot of time in the forests and on the shore, often with Ben, sometimes alone.

Hawk came and went. He was not always there, but when Hana needed him he appeared. Now and then she climbed into the sky and looked at herself, tiny on a headland or a hill. And once, out fishing with Ben, she slipped away and looked at them both, sitting close together in the dinghy, but it did not seem right and she slid back down. They pulled the dinghy up on the sand and swam in the warm sea, then walked along the beach and into the forest. She moved around to his left side so she could hold his hand.

Hawk turned in the sky. He did not mind.

THE FIRST INSTALMENT OF MAURICE GEE'S
BREATHTAKING *SALT* SERIES

Hari lives in Blood Burrow, deep in the ruined city of Belong, where he survives by courage and savagery. He is scarred from fighting, but he has a secret gift: he can speak with animals.

Pearl is from Company, the ruling families, which has conquered and enslaved Hari's people. Pampered and beautiful, she is destined for a marriage that will unite her family with that of the powerful and ambitious Ottmar. But Pearl has learned forbidden things from Tealeaf, her maid, and so the two must run.

Hari and Pearl forge an unusual alliance and become reluctant travelling companions. As the two come to grips with their strengthening powers, their quest evolves into a desperate pilgrimage to save the world from a terror beyond their greatest imaginings.

GOOL

MAURICE GEE

THE SECOND INSTALMENT OF MAURICE GEE'S BREATHTAKING *SALT* SERIES

Sixteen years have passed since Pearl from Company and Hari from Blood Burrow defeated the tyrant Ottmar. Now their children, Xantee and Lo, face an even more dangerous foe.

Hari lies gravely ill with a fragment of a strange creature wrapped around his throat, draining his life. The beast is called gool, meaning unbelonger. It is one of many, destroying the mountains and jungles of the world. Somewhere a hidden mother nourishes her gool brood – she must be found and destroyed to save Hari and the world they know.

Xantee, Lo and the brave and practical youth Duro, all of them 'speakers', set out on a perilous mission that will take them through jungles and over mountains to the ruined city of Belong, and on to Ceebeedee, where terrifying clashes with the cruel rival leaders and lurking gool await them.

PRAISE FOR *SALT*

'Gee has done remarkable work in this genre, but this is in my view the best children's book of his long career.'

David Larsen, NZ *Listener*

'A compelling tale of anger and moral development that also powerfully explores the evils of colonialism and racism.'

Publishers Weekly

PRAISE FOR *GOOL*

'Gee has proved again why he is considered a living legend in literary circles and is one of the country's most recognised authors.'

Gisborne Herald

'Even scarier than its predecessor. Gee's imagination is as fierce as ever.'

Herald on Sunday